I0603349

GROUND & POUND

MOSH SERIES BOOK 6

SUSANNA ROGERS

Bucher & Reid

Copyright © Susanna Rogers 2019
The moral right of the author has been asserted.
All rights reserved. This publication (or any part of it) may
not be reproduced or transmitted, copies, stored,
distributed or otherwise made available by any person or
entity, in any form (electronic, digital, optical, mechanical)
or by any means (photocopying, recording, scanning or
otherwise) without prior written permission from the
author.

This is a work of fiction. Names, characters, businesses,
places, events and incidents are either the products of the
author's imagination or used in a fictitious manner. Any
resemblance to actual persons, living or dead, or actual
events is purely coincidental.

Bucher & Reid

Cover by Amygdala Book Design
978-0-6484920-9-2

ALSO BY SUSANNA ROGERS

MOSH SERIES
Holler & Howl
Down & Dirty
Slash & Burn
Light & Shade
Ride & Crash
Ground & Pound

YOUNG ADULT
Infiltration (Book 1)
Regeneration (Book 2)
Validation (Book 3)

Parallax Error

DEDICATION

To Leah Shapiro
drummer in my favorite band, BRMC
who kicked the butt of serious illness and brain surgery

and to women around the world who rock and follow their
dreams

CHAPTER ONE

Holly

Maybe Morgan had forgotten. After all, a person could forget a lot of things in four years.

He'd sure done well for himself. I'd kill for a kitchen like this, immaculate in white with a huge island counter, state-of-the-art stainless steel appliances, glass splash-backs, everything a home-chef could want.

And filled with people. Everyone wanted to be your friend when you were a successful record producer, everyone except me because the last thing I needed was a friend like him.

Tentative about talking to the host, I was hanging out in the kitchen, but had no clue why these others would be here when they could be lounging on the leather sofas or relaxing by the pool. So many options, so many rooms for that matter.

Out of nowhere, Morgan Masterson came striding toward the kitchen. Like a man on a mission. Like he owned the place.

Nerves raced through my body. There was no escaping that searing gaze. As he looked at me through lowered lids,

I felt him peeling off my clothes with his eyes, layer by layer, imagining me naked, not that he'd have to try very hard because the memory might be imprinted in his mind.

I bit back my embarrassment, the memory of how stupid I'd been.

He stepped closer, his shoulders stiffening. Shit, I'd made a mistake, a big one. That was no seductive look. How could I have thought that for a second? I hoped like hell he wasn't going to kick me out or make a big deal of this.

He leaned against the counter, looking as suave as ever. "If it isn't Holly Jacobs."

I forced a smile. "Hey, Morgan."

"What brings you here tonight?"

"Oh, the same as everyone else. Happy Birthday."

I had to kiss him, so I made it quick. A peck on the cheek, nothing more but it was long enough for me to get a whiff of aftershave, something subtle and masculine. Typical.

"Thank you," he said.

"It's not every day a guy turns thirty."

He tried to blow a stray lock of hair out of his eyes, then raked a hand through to get the hair off his face, looking a lot like James Dean needing a haircut. Back when he was alive, that was.

"Thank you for reminding me," Morgan said.

"What? Thirty's not old."

He kept looking at me. I wished he wouldn't. I should keep talking, keep him distracted, then he might not realize he hadn't invited me, probably wouldn't even think about it.

"The top I'm wearing is probably thirty years old.

From the eighties." Or maybe it was nineties. I really wouldn't know. I only knew what I liked, and I liked to throw different combinations of clothes together. The top was high-necked, fitted, fabulous, and went perfectly with my ripped jeans. I probably should've worn a bra, though.

"It suits you." He held my gaze, didn't look down at my chest, thank goodness.

Surely he wouldn't mind me being here. I was just as much a part of the Frankston music scene as anyone else here. I'd played the drums for years and had managed bands too. Well, one band. It had turned into a minor disaster, mostly because I hadn't known the first thing about the music industry at the time, but they'd been desperate and I'd helped. Besides you had to be a hard ass to be a band manager. I should've known that from the start.

"I got you something," I said.

"Very kind but there was really no need. It's not that sort of party."

"What sort is it?"

He shrugged. "The kind where everyone drinks a lot and has a good time."

"I can do that!"

A smile tugged at the corners of his lips. Maybe I was winning him over after all.

"I didn't want to come empty handed." I pointed to the corner where people had left a few gifts. "Mine's the one with the big red bow. I thought, what do you get the man who has everything?"

"That's kind of why the invitation said 'no gifts' because I'd rather people didn't waste their money when there are so many better things they can do with it."

An invitation, I didn't have one of those. Think quickly, Holly.

"Oh, I didn't waste any money on you."

He raised his eyebrows. "Really?"

My face flushed. "You didn't let me finish. I thought it'd be silly for me to try to guess what you might want so rather than head to the store, I baked some cookies."

"You baked me cookies." Surprise, followed by a sly look. "Sure they're not poisoned?"

I liked his teasing tone. Two could play at that game so I planted my hands on my hips. "It might not be too late for me to drizzle some arsenic on them. If they taste like almonds, you'll know why."

"What do almonds have to do with it?"

"Arsenic tastes like bitter almonds." He stared at me, so I added, "Or so I've been told. Don't you know anything?"

"Apparently not." He sidled closer, not a lot, only enough to stake his claim. "So you've been planning and plotting this?"

I held my ground. "Hey, they're cookies. I can take them back if you like."

"I wouldn't dream of it." His expression softened. "Not when you've done something so kind. My grandma used to bake cookies for me when I was little but I can't remember the last time that happened."

"Great, I remind you of your grandma."

The words slipped out the way they always did. Still, better I reminded him of his grandmother than a drunk nineteen-year-old girl who'd practically thrown herself at him four years ago. Maybe he had forgotten after all.

"My gran is a wonderful woman and a very good cook."

"So am I." Yep, there I went, putting my foot in my mouth again. "I mean, I'm pretty good in the kitchen. Well, not that good really. I just like to cook."

"That's handy because most people like to eat." A pause, the uncomfortable kind, the kind that made me nervous, then he added. "Do you still play in the Maybe Dolls?"

"No, I'm between bands at the moment."

Between bands, between jobs, between homes. My life had become a huge 'in between' thanks to a combination of lousy circumstances. My roommate, Jess, had left our apartment to move in with Lachie, guitar player extraordinaire and a great guy to boot, absolutely the best thing that could have happened to her.

Not long after, the lease for the apartment had come up, and friends of my parents needed a house sitter while they were in Europe, someone to look after their plants and feed the fish. The timing had been too good. I couldn't argue with three months free rent, starting in a week.

Morgan cleared his throat as if he was about to make an announcement or maybe because I wasn't giving him enough attention.

He turned to me. "So did you come with someone tonight or did you crash the party on your own?"

Teasing was one thing but this was a bit close to the bone, even if I should be used to feeling unwanted.

"I didn't crash anything. I came with Jess and Lachie. Well, not *with* them exactly. They got here first."

Besides I had to be here to see The Merchants, my all-time favorite band, the sort of band I could only dream about playing with. They were playing a set later and no way could I miss them.

Drum and bass had been playing when I walked in. Now it was Post Malone. Morgan must have varied tastes.

"Great," he said. "I'm glad you didn't gatecrash."

"Absolutely not. I ... wandered."

He burst out laughing. "You wandered. So you're a wanderer? Like a burglar, do they wander in too?"

I straightened. "The door was open."

"No, it wasn't."

"Okay, it was unlocked. Same thing."

He crossed his arms. "How'd you get past Bill?"

"Oh, I... We..."

I'd known Bill for ages, had met him doing security at gigs years ago, and then Jess and Lachie had come to the door after I'd texted to say I was outside. Lachie greeted me with a big hug, said they'd been waiting for me. Made getting in pretty easy.

Morgan gave me a dull look. "You sweet-talked him, then waltzed straight in, didn't you?"

Guilty as charged, not that I'd admit it. "I didn't *waltz* anywhere."

"Of course, you *wandered*. Hmm, I'll have to be more careful from now on."

I jabbed my finger at his folded arms and he dropped them.

"Look, I'm sorry if I came in uninvited—or if you hadn't invited me—but I didn't think it'd be so terrible for me to turn up."

"Who said it was terrible?"

Such a relief. "So you don't mind?"

"Not too much." He smiled. "I just thought you might've messaged me or found some way of getting in touch. My website has a contact page. Or you could've asked Jess or Lachie. Lots of ways of reaching me."

Warmth settled inside me—at his gaze, his attention, at the fact he wanted me to call him. Maybe he'd forgotten I used to have his number, the one I'd deleted years ago. I could hope he'd forgotten all about that.

"Hey," I said. "I'm only one person. I'm not even that big."

He looked me up and down, an amused smile on his face. "Quite petite in fact."

"And I didn't think anyone would even notice me."

"I noticed you from the moment you first snuck in."

He gave me a look that was either admiring or admonishing, I couldn't tell which and had no clue where I stood with this guy. Or what I was supposed to do.

"I did not sneak. Besides, 'snuck' is not even a word. It's 'sneaked' and I didn't do that. I already told you that."

"That's right. You *wandered* in on your own, a guilty look on your face. You'd make a dreadful housebreaker or thief. Way too obvious."

Maybe it'd be better if he hadn't noticed me. Then I could hang out, watch The Merchants when they played later on, and enjoy the simple pleasures of life.

"Technically, I was on my own." I'd driven here myself after all. "But I'm not on my own anymore. I'm talking to you, and I've been mingling and being a very well behaved guest." I slumped against the counter. "Why would you want to make me feel bad?"

"I don't."

He reached for my arm, gave it a quick rub, more

friendly than suggestive yet somehow it sent a tingle up my spine. I didn't need this, didn't need his attention, and sure as hell didn't need to be reminded about anything that'd happened before.

"I was enjoying teasing you," he said.

Meanwhile I couldn't understand why he made me feel so mixed up, so defensive, so many things all at once.

"I'm not sure what's going on here," I said. "Or maybe I'm reading too much into it. You accuse me of poisoning you when I never even said thirty was old. Because it isn't. And somehow I end up being partway between your grandmother and a cat burglar."

His eyebrows went up in the middle. "Sorry, that's not how I intended any of this."

I placed a hand on my chest. "Well, I'm not the one being a Mr. Poo Poo."

A second's silence, then he burst out laughing. "I've been called a lot of things in my time but never Mr. Poo Poo."

I couldn't back out now, not after I'd said something so stupid. "I like to tell it like it is."

"Maybe more people should do that. Don't move." He stepped to one side where he reached for a clean glass from the island counter, picked up an open bottle from the ice bucket, and poured me a glass of champagne. The expensive stuff, of course.

He handed me the glass. "Here you go. I'm going to tell it like it is too, so there's no misunderstanding. You're welcome to stay as long as you like. Have a drink. Have another."

What a guy. Maybe I had him all wrong. I sipped the champagne. Magnificent. So much nicer than the cheap stuff I drank with the girls and I appreciated it all the more because this drink, my second, would be my last. The downside of driving.

"I don't usually accept a drink unless I've seen the bottle being opened," I said. "It's one of those things."

"What things?"

"Like not drinking from a glass you've left unattended. Lots of girls are careful like that. Or at least I think they are."

"Always better to be cautious but I don't think there's too much to worry about tonight. Look, I'll join you." He poured himself a glass and had a drink.

"Sorry, I didn't mean to imply you were some kind of stalker or poisoner. It's just that it's different when you're a girl. Guys don't need to watch what they wear or how much they drink. They don't check the back seat before getting into the car or lock the doors as soon as they get in, especially at night."

I'd learned a lot from my bodyguard friend, Jess, over the years and had made a few mistakes along the way too, especially with drinking too much on occasion. Yet another learning experience.

"Maybe you're right," he said. "I hadn't thought of it that way."

"Don't you have sisters?"

"Just a brother."

I sipped my champagne. "Very nice. Far as I can tell, it's not spiked. Or poisoned."

"Yep, you've got to watch out for that." Morgan leaned closer. "You know this is the longest conversation we've had in years."

Years? He remembered. Anxiety simmered in my

stomach. I shouldn't blame him for my own stupidity. But maybe I did, just a little.

I edged away. "Yes, that was a long time. An eon. An echelon."

He frowned. "An echelon?"

"That's what I said."

"An echelon is a level or rank. It doesn't have anything to do with time."

"I know that." My eyes narrowed. "Are you trying to make me look bad by pointing it out?"

He chuckled. "Holly, you're so funny."

"I wasn't trying to be funny."

"And that's exactly what makes it so amusing."

"I don't think you'll be laughing for very long."

"Why's that?"

"Chances are you're going to be seeing more of me." I cleared my throat. "We're going to be neighbors."

"What?"

"Next door neighbors."

The smile left his face. "You're kidding. I know my neighbors and neither of them has their house on the market."

"But the Ashtons are going to Europe for three months."

"Y-yes, they are." I could practically see the cogs in his head turning. "Don't tell me."

I gave him a little wave. "Yep, meet their new house sitter."

After Jess had told me Morgan's address and I'd worked this out, I'd had a bit of a panic, but I'd become used to the idea since then.

Besides, he'd be in his house and I'd be in mine. What could go wrong?

CHAPTER TWO

Morgan

My mouth fell open. Holly had to be kidding, except the look on her face told me she wasn't.

Why did the thought of having her so close make my heart stammer and my pulse race? What was going on? Hell, I'd end up a nervous wreck if I spent too much time around this woman.

I lifted the glass to my lips and drained it. "So we'll be neighbors."

"Only for three months, not forever."

"So, ah, was this another of your plans?"

She brightened. "Not a plan exactly, more of an opportunity, something that came up."

All these people in the room and somehow I kept coming back to Holly, so much so that I'd thought it better to find her and get this little discussion over with. I'd waited till I caught her on her own which hadn't been easy. She'd been mingling, maybe even avoiding me because if I was at one end of the room, she'd be at the other.

She tilted her head. "And what would be so terrible

about living next door to me anyway?"

Holly had pulled her dark wavy hair back into a ponytail that showed off her face. And her feelings. The wounded look on her face made me feel guilty.

"Nothing." I put my glass down. "It'll be fabulous."

"Yep, soon I'll be moving into my new Abbott Road Abode."

How did she come up with this stuff? Grinning, I covered my mouth to stifle a laugh.

"That was meant to sound kind of dorky, by the way." She spread her arms. "Besides, you'll be one person rattling around in your big house, and I'll be next door. I can't see why this would be a problem."

"Did I say it'd be a problem? Anyway, I'm not rattling in here."

"Isn't this place kind of big for one person?"

"Not really. I use all the rooms."

"Like the home theater?"

"I'm using it tonight. The band has set up there."

"And this enormous living area?"

I shrugged. "It's great. Perfect for a party, so we can all spread out."

"And you must have spare bedrooms."

I held her gaze, looked into those soft hazel eyes. "Maybe one day I'll be filling those bedrooms with children of my own." Unease shot through me. "Why are we even talking about this anyway?"

And how had I come up with that crap about having children? Must be something to do with turning thirty, not that I was old. That's one thing Holly was right about. But in some ways, a big birthday with a zero at the end felt like a turning point.

Her lips curved to a sly smile. "Now who's the one who doesn't like being teased?"

"Not me. I can dish it out and I can handle it."

This didn't have to be a problem. The problem was me. Partly because seeing her again made me remember the way she'd looked lying in bed, eyes closed, lips parted. She hadn't pulled up the covers, exposing the curve of her neck and those delicate shoulders. Exposing a hell of a lot more than that too. Oh, yeah, those boobs. I swallowed. Better I didn't think about them.

That night, I'd pulled the covers up, damn it, fought any urges I may have had because that would've been wrong. So wrong. Didn't that stand for something?

"Look," I said. "If we're going to be neighbors, we should make sure we get along."

"Sure, no problem," she said.

Then why did the look on her face tell me otherwise? She couldn't still be mad at me about something that'd happened years ago. Hell, I had no idea why she hadn't returned my calls, why she'd ignored me when we'd been at the same gigs and concerts. One of her bands had even used my rehearsal rooms. I'd seen the name on the booking list.

Women, who could figure them out?

Still, for now there was only one answer. "We'll call a truce. A fresh slate."

"Easy for you to say," she mumbled.

"What?" Had I heard her correctly?

"Nothing, you're right. I mean, who knows, I might need to borrow a cup of sugar."

"Why would you need to do that?"

She glared. "It's a saying."

"Well, sure, you can borrow whatever you like."

There she went again, throwing me off track. I had no clue how she did it. One of us had to take control and be mature about this. Shame it had to be me.

"Bedford is a lovely neighborhood," I said. "I think you'll like it."

Tree-lined streets, gardens filled with greenery, well kept houses, very civilized. I couldn't have been happier since I bought the place last year. The most disorderly thing that happened was kids playing on the street sometimes, and maybe I joined in on the occasional game of catch with them. Well, just the once.

Other than that, my neighbors didn't care what I did for a living. Being a record producer meant nothing to them. Perfect.

This place was so *not* rock 'n' roll. And that was exactly what I liked about it.

"I've got to agree," she said. "I did a bit of exploring, drove around for a bit. I just wanted to check out how far to the nearest store, that kind of thing. Nothing to do with any planning or plotting on my part."

"I wouldn't think that for a moment."

She glanced around the room. "Is it always like this at your place? Wild parties every night?"

"This is the first party I've had since I moved in. Probably won't have another one till I'm forty."

"Ooh, forty." She smiled or maybe smirked. "Just around the corner."

"It's ten years off! How is that around the corner?"

She raised her eyebrows. "You're turning into a Mr. Sensitive."

Yet another name I'd never been called before, and so

ridiculous it made me smile. Was she sensitive too? She was certainly a hoot.

"This isn't a wild party," I said. "Not for these people."

"I'm not so sure. It's got all the hallmarks. I mean, look at all these cool hipster types. You'll have a live band playing soon. The Merchants, the biggest, coolest band in the whole country. And there's a heap of people smoking dope outside."

Which was not my thing but seemed to be part and parcel of the music industry. If I'd excluded anyone who'd ever dabbled in drugs from the party, there'd probably only be about three people here.

Meanwhile I found my work so engrossing that I wasn't interested in smoking pot or snorting coke. A few beers was all it took to keep me happy or, in this case, a glass of champagne and some special company.

"There's something I wanted to say to you..." Her voice trailed off.

Good or bad, I could handle it. "Sure, go ahead."

"Look, I'm a huge fan of The Merchants. And, okay, I'm not the only one so that's probably not news."

"I love the band too. Can't deny it."

"That first album is still their best, in my opinion anyway, and that's largely down to you. You did a brilliant job with that record, really captured a rawness and vibrancy. I'd go as far as to say The Merchants couldn't have got that kickstart without you. You were part of their sound. Instrumental in it."

"And that's without playing an actual instrument!"

She laughed, such a lovely sound. Meanwhile it left me wondering if her admiration from a professional point of view was all I'd get.

"And I'm sure you'll do a fabulous job with this next album," she added, making it sound like there was a 'but' coming. "That's it. That's what I wanted to say."

"Very nice of you. Thank you."

"And now I'm going to get some fresh air."

She turned and walked away, ponytail swinging, hips encased in those tight jeans. How could a woman look so alluring when she was so covered up?

Maybe I could do with some fresh air too. I tried not to look like I was staring at her butt as I wandered outside. I could be a wanderer too.

A whisper of wind edged through the air, cool air, which was saying something for Nevada in the summer. Maybe the pool helped to keep the temperature down a little. I liked having one even if I didn't use it much. I felt cooler just looking at it, and at night the reflections of water rippling on the patio ceiling never ceased to amaze me.

Holly bounded up to Jess and Lachie, who waved for me to join them.

"Yo, Morgan," he said.

"When are you guys going to start playing?" I asked.

"Soon."

Anyone who'd played in a band knew that 'soon' meant anywhere between five minutes and five hours. I didn't want to be pushy, not tonight and not with the other issues the guys were dealing with. They could go at their own pace.

Holly put her hands on her hips, a teasing smile on her lips. "You're not following me around and stalking me, are you?"

So much for my relaxing thoughts. "Hey, it's my party."

Jess looked around. "Did you say something about a stalker?"

Holly placed a hand on her arm. "Relax, Jess. I was joking. No need to be in bodyguard mode all the time."

"No problem. I won't beat anyone up unless they deserve it."

Jess couldn't even say that with a straight face. Holly cracked up, so comfortable with her friends that I wondered if I should leave her to it. Or maybe I should be the consummate host and introduce her to some people.

"Have you met Joel?" I asked.

Holly nodded. "Yeah, we used to play in The Poisonberries together."

"Really?"

"He's an awesome bass player, one of the best I've played with. Maybe the best ever. Of the people I've played with, that is."

"Yeah, he's definitely got the groove but I don't know if he's up there with the likes of Flea or John Entwistle."

She raised her finely arched eyebrows. "John who?"

"John Entwistle, from a little band called The Who." A smile twitched at the corners of my lips. "You might've heard of them."

Holly frowned. "Of course, I've heard of them but I didn't know this was supposed to be a history lesson."

She looked cute when she pouted. Reminded me of Naomi, so young, so lovely, so determined to dump me and find someone better. There's always something about first love that stays with you. You'd think I'd have learned my lesson after that but I went on to make the same mistakes over again.

I cleared my throat. "Hard to avoid a bit of history if we're talking about greatest bass players who ever existed."

"I'm just saying it was before my time."

"Before mine too." I found it hard not to sound defensive.

"Okay, I didn't think you went back as far as the sixties."

Lachie grinned, placing a hand on my shoulder. "Don't worry, Morgan, I don't think thirty's old. You've got your whole life ahead of you. Or most of it, anyway."

Holly laughed, her smile reaching her eyes, her face lighting up. Her entire disposition had changed now she was talking to friends instead of me. That bothered me, not because I didn't want her to be happy, but because she'd been trying to avoid me earlier.

"Very funny, guys," I said, deadpan. "Holly, I suppose you've heard more than your share of drummer jokes."

"One or two."

"Some people in the industry don't even think drummers are musicians," I added.

She narrowed her gaze. "I can't imagine what that's supposed to mean. Drummers are the backbone of a band. Just because percussion is underrated doesn't mean it's not important, critical to a band even. And you of all people should know that."

I held my hands out. "Hey, I said 'some people'. Not me. I'd never say something like that. I don't think drummers are just people who hang out with musicians, no way."

An old joke but a good one. It made Lachie laugh

while Holly stood there glaring.

"In case you're wondering…" she began.

"About what?" I asked.

"I'm pretty good on the drums nowadays. Much better than the last time you saw me, whenever that was."

The memories made me cringe. The first time I'd seen her play, she'd been abysmal. The second time hadn't been much better. She'd improved. It would've been hard not to.

I should change the subject. I didn't want to insult her. Lachie leaned across to whisper something in Jess's ear, then pressed a kiss to her temple, tender and touching.

I stepped closer to Holly. "So you know Lachie pretty well?"

"Yep, I wasn't sure about him at first but I am now. Despite the fact he plays in my favorite band and he'd just started dating my best friend, he didn't make such a good impression."

"Why's that?"

Her eyes narrowed as she sipped her champagne. "He referred to my Gretsch drum kit as a mother of toilet seat."

A classic set-up in pearlescent white that had nothing to do with bathrooms and everything to do with good taste. I could picture her behind that kit and was glad she'd upgraded from the cheap borrowed one she'd started off with.

"It might've been just an observation," I offered.

"Nope, it sounded rather like a drummer joke."

I rolled my eyes. "What kind of person would make one of those?"

"Cooper's a brilliant drummer," she said. "His

drumming really drives The Merchants' songs."

He was also one of the reasons the other band members didn't make drummer jokes, not anymore. Everyone in the band had become protective of him.

A pang shot through my gut. If you didn't have your health, you didn't have much at all.

"The Merchants aren't looking for another drummer." The words slipped out before I could stop myself. No doubt they'd be looking for a new drummer soon but that was none of my business.

"I didn't say they were." Holly frowned. "Why would you even say that?"

Good question. "I was making a joke."

"Really? I'd love to meet him, Cooper, that is." She looked up at me, her hazel eyes widening.

"Is that a request?"

She smiled. "Maybe."

"He's here somewhere." I looked around but Nick was closer, right behind me in fact, so I reached for his arm. "Hey, Nick, there's someone I'd like to introduce you to."

"Sure thing." He shook back his long hair, stepped right over toward Holly. "And you must be…"

She stretched out her arm for a handshake. "Holly."

He took her hand and leaned across to kiss her on the cheek. "Lovely to meet you."

Her whole face lit up, not like when she'd given me the world's quickest birthday kiss earlier. I hadn't seen anything light up then.

I nudged Nick. "Hey, when did you get to be so polite?"

"I'm always polite, dude." He put his arm around Lily, now standing beside him. "And this is Lily."

More politeness. I should have done the introductions but he'd beaten me to it.

"Lovely to meet you," Holly said. "And congratulations. I heard you guys got married."

Nick and Lily were both beaming. Good for them.

"Ah, but the honeymoon is over." Nick became more serious, his arm slipping away from Lily. "We've got a truckload of recording ahead of us. Loads of work to do."

The Merchants' new album was the project I'd been waiting for, but I had a lot of other bookings, including a trip to Phoenix the week after next.

Holly edged closer to Lily. "I saw some pictures of your dress online. Absolutely gorgeous."

"Hey, are you guys talking about the record?" Lachie asked Nick.

I didn't want to talk shop but somehow found myself debating the benefits of using a tube pre-amp for the mikes or a solid state pre-amp for the vocals. This kind of thing seemed to happen when bands had a new record coming up.

Even though I didn't think myself qualified to join in on the wedding talk, I listened in to the girls with one ear while trying to steer the guys in the direction of more sociable topics. I noticed Holly had her phone in her hand.

"How are things going at The Swamp?" I asked Nick. "The bar has got to be ready to re-open soon."

"Soon." He turned to Holly. "You must've been to The Swamp?"

"Huh, sorry?" She looked up from her phone, bit her lip, then cleared her throat. "Yeah, I've played a couple of gigs there."

"You've got to come to the grand opening," Nick said.

"I'll let you know as soon as I have the date."

"Thanks." Her face pale, she spoke to Jess, both of them suddenly serious. Nick said something I didn't quite catch. I did catch Holly saying, "Honestly, it's fine." Then, "Excuse me, I've got to go."

What was going on? No way could I leave it at that.

"I'll walk you to the door." I ushered her through the crowd, waiting till we were in the relative quiet of the hall. "Is everything okay?"

She stopped, her jaw clenched. "I just got a text message from a friend. He's been in a car crash."

"Oh, no."

"He's at Frankston General getting checked over and insists there's nothing wrong or broken but his partner, Ian, is away for the weekend. I can't leave him there on his own, not after he texted me."

I reached for her hand. "Is there anything I can do?"

She shook her head, looked down, and frowned. "Damn it, my phone just ran out of juice."

"Just as well you got the message first."

"Yeah. Look, I need to go."

We strode through the front door past Bill. Holly's car was parked out front.

She opened the door of the Honda, then looked up. "Thanks for…"

"For what?"

"I was going to say 'for inviting me'."

I shot her a wry smile. As soon as I got inside, I'd get her number from Jess and text her later to make sure she was okay.

"Goodnight." I watched her leave.

I should've asked her when she was moving in next door. One thing was for sure. I'd be seeing more of her.

CHAPTER THREE

Holly

I pulled up outside the Ashton place, my home for the next three months. I'd already been here earlier this morning while some of my old furniture was being delivered, not that I'd need it while I was here but it had to be stored somewhere and they had plenty of space in their garage.

Walking to the back of the car, I pulled open the rear door, marveling at how I'd accumulated so many boxes of … stuff. What's more, there were at least two more carloads after this.

I glanced across at Morgan's house. No peep from next door, no reason there should be, and certainly no good reason I should be thinking about him. He'd messaged me a couple of times to tell me how much he liked the cookies I'd baked and also offering to help me move. Very neighborly of him but I hadn't wanted to impose.

I got to work, carrying the first of the boxes into the house, deciding that the workout my thighs would be getting today could only be a good thing.

When I came out, who should be outside leaning against my Honda with his arms folded? My heart stuttered, probably from all the exercise.

"Morning," I said when I reached the car.

"Need a hand?" Morgan asked.

I thought about the boxes and about my sore muscles. Thought about the way Morgan made me want to grab him and push him at the same time. Thought about saying yes.

Instead I said, "I'll be fine, thanks."

"I heard all the commotion with the delivery guys."

The 'delivery guys' were two friends with a U-Haul who'd moved the larger pieces of furniture for me. After I'd stayed with Michael at the Emergency Room that night, he'd insisted this was the least he and Ian could do, not that I thought he owed me.

Unfortunately I'd slept in this morning and the two of them had to leave to get ready for a wedding, which meant we ran out of time so they could only move the bigger items. I'd insisted it was fine. I could take the smaller boxes and the musical instruments myself after all.

"We didn't make too much noise, did we?" I asked.

He shrugged. "I saw you through the window."

"Were you being nosy and spying on me?"

I wasn't sure why I came out with things like this but it simply seemed to happen when Morgan was around.

Besides, I might be a bit nosy myself. Something had happened after I'd left his party last weekend, an incident with Cooper where he'd ended up in the ER the same night I'd been there with Michael. Unlike Michael, Cooper hadn't been discharged quickly. It made me wonder how Morgan was doing after that too.

"I was trying to sleep," he said.

Okay, now I felt bad but tried to sound upbeat. "I guess you're awake now."

"Guess I am."

He didn't look like a guy who'd been forced out of bed on a Saturday. His brown hair had that slightly tousled look that seemed to be a permanent fixture for him. Dark hair, dark eyes, the guy was overloaded with mystery, the kind of guy who'd been around and knew a thing or two.

He stepped over to the back of the car and peered inside. "Amazing how much you can get into one of these things."

"It's a Honda Fit."

"I know."

"The seats fold right down. Leaves me with heaps of space."

He straightened. "Yep."

"I needed enough room for the drum kit but didn't want a big car." Which was now filled with heavy boxes. I chewed my lip, trying not to stare at Morgan's muscular physique, the broad shoulders, and strong chest. "Actually I'd love a hand. Please."

He stood there, doing that dark-and-mysterious thing. I had no idea why he made me so nervous that I ended up rambling.

"It was nice of you to offer," I added.

"No problem." Leaning inside, he pulled two boxes forward, tested their weight, then handed me the lighter one. "Between the two of us, we'll get this done in no time."

After we got back to the car, Morgan said, "I'm surprised Jess isn't helping."

"She's got something planned today."

I hadn't wanted to inconvenience her and Lachie so I'd insisted I had the situation under control, which may have been a slight overstatement.

Besides, Jess had done so much for me, practically since the first day we'd met at high school.

Morgan gave me a quizzical look. "Are you one of these independent types?"

"No, it's just everyone else was busy. And I do most stuff for myself."

"Sounds like independence to me."

I thought about it. "I prefer to think of it as self-sufficiency."

After my experience with Jason, I'd learned to do nearly everything on my own. Much better than depending on some unreliable jerk and ending up in a mess.

"Do you have a boyfriend or brother or someone who could help?" Morgan asked.

"A brother?" I laughed. "Yeah, I've got one of those but he's pretty useless."

The only person he ever helped was himself. Yet somehow he'd managed to get away with it when we were growing up while I'd been saddled with most of the jobs, and the criticisms that seemed to go along with that.

"Just wondering, that's all." Morgan pulled forward a box. "My family's all over the place. My brother's in Chicago, Mom's in Denver, and my dad lives out in the desert."

Meanwhile I was glad my parents were happy with each other because my mother never seemed happy with me.

As Morgan reached for the big suitcase, probably the

heaviest item of all, I was grateful for his presence, his help, those muscles. I took a deep breath, forcing myself not to think about that physique.

We emptied the boxes from the back of the Fit, as well as a couple on the front passenger seat. After we had them inside the house, I slammed the rear door of the hatchback shut, wiped my palms on my pants, and shook Morgan's hand.

"One down, two more to go," I said.

"Sorry? You mean you've got two more carloads of gear to bring over?"

I nodded. "Including the drum kit, but I can take care of it. You've already done so much."

He raised his eyebrows. "I can't leave you to do all that on your own."

"Sure you can."

I swallowed. Did that sound as dumb to him as it did to me?

"I don't mind helping," he said. "We can go together in your car and I'll carry the heavier items."

Together. In my car. How was I supposed to breathe with him so close and in such a confined space? I was having a hard enough time keeping my head together around him as it was.

"But you'll be taking up valuable space," I blurted out.

"Sorry, *I'll* be taking up space?"

"Yeah, you'll take up the whole front seat and I can fit a bunch of boxes in there."

Morgan pointed toward his place. "Tell you what. I'll take my car and you can take yours. Two cars, one trip, much easier."

"Oh." It sounded too good to be true. "When you put

it that way…"

"When I put it that way *what?*"

"Yes. Did I forget to say yes?" I reached for his hand, took it into mine, felt the softness of his skin and something else, a warmth deep in my belly. "I forgot something else too. Thank you so much."

He glanced down at my hand. And his. "No problem."

I let go of his fingers, slipping my hand away and hoping he hadn't noticed, though the chances of that were slim. I had no idea where all this anxiety was coming from.

"Also," I said. "My handcart broke so I need all the help I can get."

"I'll bring mine."

"A man with a handcart sounds like a pretty sexy offer to me."

He laughed, thank goodness, because my words sounded so wrong, even to me.

I cleared my throat. "You can follow me in your car."

He kept looking at me, only I couldn't tell if it was admiringly or as if I was an idiot. A fresh wave of nerves rolled over me.

I threw my hands up. "What are you waiting for?"

"I'll get my keys." He turned and walked away.

Five minutes later we were on our way, me in my little Honda and him in his huge Range Rover. When we reached the apartment, I pulled the door open and shuffled inside, where my trusty Gretsch kit took center stage in the middle of the living room. Boxes lined the walls, my old guitar lying in its case on top of them.

The memories hit me all over again. The place hadn't been the same since Jess had left, silent and empty. She'd always been a wonderful roommate but now she was moving on in life, which was exactly what I had to do too.

Morgan placed a hand on my shoulder. "Are you okay?"

I nodded. "Yeah, sure. There's even more stuff here than I'd thought."

"We'll manage."

I should've culled instead of accumulated, yet another of my faults. Still, that was nothing compared to my mistakes with men. Falling for a teacher had been a big blunder, followed by falling in love with a guy who couldn't control his temper. One disaster after another.

Morgan got to work right away, handing me a box and taking one for himself before leading the way to the cars. I wandered behind, happy to follow for once, happy with the view. How could I not have noticed that tight butt before? Not that I was looking but I couldn't help it if he was walking in front of me.

He opened the rear door of the Range Rover and loaded in the first of the boxes.

"Whoa," I said.

"Pardon?"

I pointed to the interior where the leather seats had been folded down. "Why do you even need a house? You could practically live in there."

He smiled. "Not quite."

I looked across at my car. "Still the Honda Fit packs a punch. Much better value in terms of space and economy if you look at it pound for pound."

"You sound like a boxing commentator."

I laughed. "Sorry, maybe I've been hanging around Jess too long. She's into her UFC."

Morgan took charge of loading my stuff into the cars,

and I didn't argue because he had a good handle on spatial awareness. Maybe it was a guy thing. For once, I didn't mind handing over the reins to someone else, maybe because I felt I could trust him. When it came to moving house, anyway.

Several trips later, I couldn't help but notice he'd left plenty of space in the Range Rover.

"So you'll be taking my drum kit?" I asked.

"If that's okay."

I sucked in a deep breath. "Of course."

Morgan led the way back to the Ashton place. We unloaded the drum kit first, leaving it in the living room for the time being. Then we kept going, box after box till both cars had been emptied and the hallway was full. Standing room only.

"This one's heavy." Morgan deposited the final box inside the front door. "What've you got in here?"

"My record collection."

I crouched down, pulled out a few, admiring the shiny covers, thinking about my favorite artists.

Morgan stood there. "You can tell a lot about a person from their record collection."

"Go on then."

He squatted down beside me and leaned across, his arm brushing against mine as he flipped through the collection. Meanwhile, I waited. Nervously. Warmth settled deep in my belly, my senses on edge.

"Eclectic," he said.

"One word." I threw my hands up. "That's it?"

"Yep. You've got some old Motown, a bit of heavy metal, a hip-hop collection most people would kill for, and you've also got Neil Diamond and Taylor Swift. What the hell am I supposed to make of that?"

"It belonged to my grandma."

"Your grandmother is a Taylor Swift fan?"

"No, silly, Neil Diamond." I screwed up my face. "You know, it kind of gets worse."

"Why's that?"

"There's more, loads more. Most of my music is on iTunes."

He smiled, holding my gaze as he got to his feet. "I should get going."

I stood a little too quickly so he reached for my arm to steady me, his grip firm and reassuring. Not a lot of space in here with all these boxes, yet somehow claustrophobic had never felt so good, so enticing, so alluring. I had to stop myself from thinking that way.

"Thanks." I let out a breath. "Can I get you a drink? You must be thirsty."

"Okay."

He followed me to the kitchen, a country style room decked out with lots of timber and old fashioned warmth. I filled two glasses with water, handed him one, watched him sit down and drink. Somehow I'd liked it better when we'd been cramped together in the hallway.

"What?" he asked.

"Nothing." I gulped back some water, stopped staring, and pulled up a chair. "Can I ask you something?"

"Sure."

"It's about Cooper. Is he going to be all right?"

A pause, a long one. "Jess told you?"

I nodded.

Pain glimmered in Morgan's eyes. "He's not ready to make his illness public yet, but it's only a matter of time."

I reached for his hand, gave it a squeeze. "I'm sorry. He's your friend."

A pang cut through my heart—for Cooper, for his friends, his family, for everyone who mattered.

I wondered if The Merchants would be looking for a new drummer, yet it seemed so selfish that I barely dared to think it.

"What about the other guys in the band?" I asked. "They must be gutted. What are they going to do?"

"Who knows?"

It must've been a shock for Morgan too. "And you? How are you doing?"

He held my gaze then nodded. "I'm doing okay, Holly."

"Are you getting hungry? I can throw something together for lunch."

He drank the rest of his water. "No, I've got a booking at the studio in an hour and a busy couple of weeks ahead."

"Y-yeah, so do I."

"Really?"

"Oh, you know, settling in here." And looking for a band, I didn't mention that. "I'm hoping to get some work at Charlie's."

"Selling musical instruments?"

"No, I'll be in the CD section." Filling in when Charlie needed me, which wasn't the same as having a proper job. "And you?"

"I've got lots of recording scheduled, including a trip to Phoenix."

Sounded exciting. "Phoenix?"

Morgan shrugged. "Yeah, they want to record at home

in a garage. The guy thinks he's Dave Grohl."

I smiled. "Another of my favorites."

"And there's the opening of The Swamp." He got to his feet. "I might see you there."

"Sure, Nick texted me an invite."

He grinned. "If he'd forgotten, you could've just wandered in."

"I've never been much of a wanderer."

For a moment, I thought he might suggest we go to The Swamp together. Excitement tingled inside me, my breath catching in my throat. What would it be like to spend more time with Morgan? What might happen next?

"Give me a yell if you need a hand with anything." He turned and left so I jumped up to walk him to the door.

"Thanks again." I held the door open as I watched him leave, and I didn't feel a single thing. Or barely a single thing. Hardly anything at all.

CHAPTER FOUR

Morgan

A lot had happened while I'd been in Phoenix. My new neighbor for one thing. Holly had been next door for two weeks and I'd only seen her that one time, worst luck. Cooper had been in the hospital and out again, pretending he was all right, acting as if everything would be fine.

And here we all were, back at The Swamp again, only the place had never looked so good. It still had an element of the old grunge with the wooden bar top that'd been refurbished but still had initials carved into it. The entire room had been rearranged and the bar repositioned. For the better.

I had to hand it to Nick. He'd done an excellent job.

Holly came bounding up to me, her smile taking over the room and maybe a little piece of my heart. She'd let her hair down tonight, curls framing her face and brushing against her shoulders. She wore a leopard print jacket with a fluffy collar that looked almost sensible on her. Matching shoes too. Cute. Meanwhile the summer dress hanging off her tiny frame made her look petite.

"Isn't it a bit warm for a jacket?" I asked her.

"Nope."

And who was I to argue? Maybe it was better she kept herself covered or I'd end up staring at her boobs. I swallowed. I remembered them well, maybe too well.

"You're back," she said.

"I wouldn't miss tonight for anything. This is a big deal for Nick."

"I can't wait till they have bands playing here again."

Though still a big empty space, the band room had been brought up to date with acoustic panels to improve the sound and a mural the new bass player, Joel, had painted that transformed the place.

As we were looking that way, Cooper wandered into the band room on his own. Something didn't seem right. Should I join him? That didn't feel right either. He wouldn't want my pity, but sometimes I couldn't help myself.

I glanced across at Holly. She'd seen him too.

"I'm sorry about your friend," she said.

"Yeah, me too." Something about her response touched me.

"People have been talking, all kinds of rumors going around."

"Cooper's starting to be more open about it now." My throat tightened. "In some ways, he's handling it better than the other guys."

Someone pushed past behind Holly, so she stepped forward, her arm brushing against mine. I had the sudden urge to take her into my arms but pushed the idea away. That'd be a great way to get my face slapped, and I wouldn't blame her.

"What's Cooper going to do?" she asked. "I mean, the

band is supposed to be recording and then there's the Salt Flats Festival."

"It's one thing at a time, I guess. With the new album, we can slow things down, work around him, take our time if we need to."

"I'm sure you'll do a fabulous job."

I smiled wanly. "Thanks."

"The Flats is different, though. Not something you can delay. What if The Merchants have to cancel? I mean, they're headlining and everything."

I gritted my teeth. "It won't come to that."

Cooper's condition only served to remind me of my own mortality. Normally I went about my day-to-day life and didn't think about things too hard because I had more than enough to keep me occupied. Then, when I was least expecting it, I'd think about him and it'd sting, the vulnerability, the inescapability of it.

"I hope he's looking after himself," Holly said.

"He is. He hasn't touched a drop of alcohol in the past two years. Lives the life of a saint compared to the rest of us."

"Well, people in the music industry aren't exactly known for being saintly."

"True. It's tough, though. There are other drummers but there's only one Cooper."

Glancing through the crowd, I saw Ginger pausing outside the band room, then going in. Though they hadn't been seeing each other long, she'd take care of Cooper, or at least I thought she would. Must be gut wrenching for the two of them.

Holly cleared her throat. "So The Merchants are looking for a replacement?"

I nodded. "Pretty much."

"They need a new drummer."

A question or a statement, I wasn't sure which. Holly's voice trailed off. Surely she couldn't be thinking what I thought she was thinking. The girl was crazy but she couldn't be that crazy.

She looked down. "Sorry if that sounds mercenary."

Not what I'd been thinking at all. I still couldn't get my head around it. Holly Jacobs? In The Merchants? In what alternate universe would that possibly happen?

She lifted her gaze. "I feel for Cooper, truly I do, but I can't let an opportunity like this pass by."

"What opportunity?"

"The chance to play with The Merchants."

"You can't be serious."

Her eyes filled with hurt, her expression pained. Guilt washed over me because I didn't want to blow her dreams apart, but at the same time, this was so nuts I didn't even know where to start. And now there was no turning back, not after I'd scoffed at her so openly.

"Of course I am," she said.

"You think you could play with The Merchants?"

Defiance blazed in her eyes. "What's so hard to believe about that? Is it because I'm a girl?"

"No."

I covered my mouth. It had nothing to do with her gender and everything to with the fact she couldn't play drums to save her life. But I couldn't say something so hurtful. Nerves jittered in my stomach. I had to think of something.

"Look," I said. "Those guys have cemented their position in the rock world whereas you haven't been playing very long, only a year or two."

"Over four."

"Sorry?"

"I've been playing for over four years and I might not have been very good to begin with, but everyone's got to start somewhere. That first band was in trouble and I helped them out."

"I thought you started off as their manager."

"Well, yeah, I offered to manage them even though I didn't know what I was doing. I admit that part. But then they were touring and the drummer sold the guitarist's Stratocaster and amp to buy drugs and ran off with his junkie girlfriend."

I'd heard the story before. Same thing had happened to The Merchants years ago. "Why is it always the drummer?"

"I guarantee you it would never be me."

"That's not what I meant."

"Those guys needed me. We were stuck in the middle of nowhere and they didn't have anyone else. I had to learn the drums in a hurry. I didn't lose my shit about it, though. I did my best. Did pretty good in the end. My drumming has improved incredibly since you last saw me play."

Panic simmered in my veins. No way could I get out of this without insulting her. Also no way did I believe her drumming was anywhere near The Merchants' standards. She'd have to keep drumming for another twenty years for that to happen.

She glared. "I was still a teenager. I'm not the same person I was back then."

I held a hand out. "I'm sure you're not."

"You're not going to help me, are you?"

I didn't want to answer that.

Her eyes narrowed. "You think I'm some drunk nineteen-year-old you can take advantage of? I made a mistake. Lots of people make mistakes when they're young."

"Excuse me?"

Was she talking about what I thought she was talking about? I'd taken care of her, not taken advantage of her. And what on earth did that have to do with her drumming for The Merchants?

She jabbed a finger at my chest. "You can't judge me for what happened when I was a teenager because, let me tell you, you don't exactly come up squeaky clean after that either. What's more, you were a grown man who should've known better. So what's *your* excuse?"

"Sorry, you've lost me."

I looked around, suddenly conscious of the scene she was causing, but no one had noticed. Yet. I wiped the perspiration from my brow, wondering how the hell she was making me break out into a sweat.

She scrunched her little hands into fists. "You might be a fancy record producer but that doesn't have to mean anything to me. I don't need your help or your approval or anything from you."

"Holly, you need to calm down."

Absolutely the wrong thing to say. No one in the history of mankind had ever calmed down after being told to do so. I pressed my eyes shut for a moment, hoping this would all go away.

"Some neighbor you turned out to be." She stepped closer, lowering her voice so I had to concentrate to hear.

"You sound like my mother. Telling me I'm not good enough."

"That's not what I said." And what did her mother have to do with anything?

"It's what you're thinking, though."

True. I swallowed, tried to think quickly.

I lowered my voice too. "I think … those guys are out of your league. They're stars. They play stadiums."

She stood so close yet she couldn't have been further away. Her mind was somewhere else—possibly off with the fairies with the way she was talking—while her petite body was right here in front of me.

Petite and pretty, soft and warm. So close, so unattainable. So enticing, so frustrating. What was this woman doing to me?

"They weren't always out of my league," she said.

"Sorry, you've lost me."

"They're in a different *echelon* now. See, I do know what the word means." I nodded and she continued. "But they used to be regular guys playing shitty little gigs for next-to-no money."

"Well, they're not regular guys anymore. Not in that sense."

"But they used to be. That's my point. They proved you can make things happen if you really want to. Lots of cool stuff comes out of this town. People do their own thing, create their own art and music and writing." She paused. "And if those guys could stick it out, so can I."

I raked a hand through my hair. How could she be so right and so wrong all at the same time? You needed perseverance to succeed in this industry and a bit of luck and a lot of other things, including talent, the one thing she was missing.

Yet, somehow I couldn't help but admire her tenacity, her gumption, maybe even her naivety. This was all wrong. I shouldn't be admiring anything about her.

"Holly…"

Holly what? What could I say to her that wouldn't be a huge insult?

She gave me a pointed stare. "I don't need people like you holding me back. I got this far on my own and when I want something, I don't let anything stand in my way."

I held my hands out. "I'm not standing in your way. You can do anything you like, stay leave, whatever."

"I'm not leaving."

"Fine."

"I'm having a fabulous time. If anyone's leaving, it should be you."

I placed a hand on my chest. "Me?"

"I have friends here Mr. Hot Shot Record Producer, and I don't let my friends down."

She turned away. Gone in an instant, weaving her way through the crowd, the dark curls of her hair bouncing. Yep, she was the sort of person who bounced. Her teeth gleamed as she turned to smile at someone. Damn it, why did she have to look so gorgeous?

Two could play at that game. If she was having a *fabulous time,* so was I.

Cooper and Ginger stepped out of the band room and wove their way through the crowd. If I wasn't mistaken, they were heading for the door trying to make a quiet exit. I couldn't blame them. Life was short and they should be together.

I headed for the bar where the manager Tara had lined

up shooters for the guests. I had three, got right into the spirit of things, then followed it up with a beer.

Two guys I'd done some recording with last year came up to talk to me. I laid no claim to being a great hip-hop producer and I'd told them that before we started recording, but they'd insisted. They'd wanted a sound with an edge and I gave it to them. Now they were mixing with the likes of Travis Scott and Chance the Rapper.

I finished the beer and grabbed another. Holly was at the other end of the room, not that I was looking. Not my fault that leopard print thing she was wearing stood out so much and kept catching my eye.

Time to mingle. I knew enough people here. Time to drink. I did that too. Nothing like a cold beer—or several—to take the edge off the evening.

I found Austin, The Merchants' ex bass player and also the architect for the bar's refurbishment, so I let him know much I liked what he'd done with the place. I tried to keep the conversation coherent because there was a slim chance the booze was getting to me. Normally I didn't drink too much. Didn't like the hangovers. Tonight I didn't care.

Austin left to talk to someone else. Holly had meandered to the middle of the room, in the midst of an animated discussion with Joel, probably trying to talk her way into getting an audition. Good luck to her. Probably also telling him what a bastard I was.

I'd been tactful tonight. Hadn't said what I really thought. It wasn't as if *I* was the problem.

Hell, maybe Holly was still the same crazy-ass teenager I'd met all those years ago. As crazy as Naomi, my first true love, who dumped me for someone better after three years together because Masterson's Studio wasn't making any money when I first started.

Second true love turned out even worse. Juliet had made a pretense of being a good person with integrity. Until she'd shown her true colors. It still sent a pang through my heart. Every time.

Nick shoved a beer into my hand. "Morgan, you look thirsty."

I chugged back some beer. "You've done an amazing job with this place."

We started a heavy discussion about music, which was inevitable with two guys like us. People came up to talk to us, probably also inevitable when we both knew nearly everyone in the room.

After a while, the crowd thinned. How had that happened? Must be getting late. Might even be time to get going soon. Which was what I said to Nick. Or what I thought I'd said.

He slung his arm around me. "You might've had too much to drink."

"That was the aim, wasn't it?"

We both laughed. At least I wasn't stupid enough to drive home. I'd take a cab. Even in my drunken state, I could work that much out.

Holly came up. To Nick, not me. She'd taken off that leopard thing, showing off the strappy dress and her pretty shoulders. Very pretty. And absolutely none of my business.

Then there was the creamy skin and a hint of cleavage, which drew my eyes to those boobs. My skin tightened, one part of my flesh in particular.

I was a man. I was weak. I wanted to reach out and grab her, take her into my arms.

"Good luck with the bar." She gave him a kiss on the cheek. Looked like she was leaving.

"Hey," he said. "Maybe you can give Morgan a ride. He's had a few too many."

She smiled through gritted teeth. Didn't say 'yes'. Didn't say 'no' either. Probably didn't know how to get out of it.

I shuffled alongside her, tossing up what to do. I sure as hell wasn't getting into the car with her if she didn't want me there. If I was in the passenger seat, we'd be so close I could reach out and touch her, and I couldn't do that.

"You don't have to do this." I stood, swaying when we reached the door.

"Good." She stopped and straightened. "Because you'd take up too much valuable space."

That sounded familiar somehow but I couldn't quite place it.

"About tonight's conversation." She gave me a dirty look. "Joel was a lot more helpful than you were. Maybe you don't understand how much this means to me. It's the dream I've never even allowed myself to have."

"I'm sorry."

Sorry I'd said anything, sorry the subject had come up, sorry I'd drunk too much, a huge goddamn list of things to be sorry for.

Her lips thinned. "I'm not going to let you crap all over my parade."

She stalked away. I hoped she'd turn around, tell me she'd changed her mind, maybe even smile. Just a small smile to let me know I hadn't completely blown it.

No such luck. Looked like I'd be walking home.

CHAPTER FIVE

Holly

This wasn't the first time I'd been in one of Morgan Masterson's rehearsal rooms and it wouldn't be the last.

Because The Merchants were going to need to rehearse with their new drummer, and that was going to be me. I hoped.

Man, it was hard to exude confidence when I was sitting behind the drum kit facing my musical idols. And Joel. Maybe his presence would be enough to give me a boost. We'd played together before and if he could do this, so could I.

Joel leaned his bass against the amp and came over behind the drum kit. "How're you doing?"

"Fabulous." A tiny lie.

A fresh wave of nerves rolled through my body. I hadn't even realized how much I wanted this until the opportunity had come up. I could make it big, be part of something, prove to myself and my mom that I was a success.

Joel gave my shoulder a squeeze. "Just be yourself and do your thing. It'll be fine."

I nodded. Fine to go back to my day job which wasn't even a proper job, because I was still waiting to fill in for the staff at Charlie's if they got sick. Fine to go back to the Ashton house which, though a mansion by my standards, was only somewhere to stay in the short-term. Yep, everything was peachy-keen-dandy-fine, couldn't be better. My stomach sank. Big-time.

"Good luck," he said in a low voice and turned.

Each of us had settled into our own corners of the rehearsal studio, though my corner was by far the biggest because the kit took up so much space.

I sucked in a deep breath. It all came down to who you knew, and I'd used all my connections to get here. Joel had been my first port of call. Then Jess and Lachie. Added to that, for some reason I didn't even understand, Nick seemed to have warmed to me from the start.

One more thing I needed to deal with. I cleared my throat, tried to attract their attention. "Hey, guys, I hope it's okay if I ask. Is Cooper okay with these auditions? I wanted to make sure."

Silence, then Lachie spoke up. "It was his idea, actually. We'd been putting it off."

A reason for me to not feel so bad. Except I did, and no doubt they felt a truckload worse. He was their friend, after all.

The other guys seemed to have something to adjust or fiddle with—guitars, bass, amps, pedals—while I sat with my back straight behind the drum kit, rolling my shoulders in an effort to iron out the knots, while trying to look cool. And failing.

A knock on the door made me jump. The others barely lifted an eyebrow as Morgan walked in. Or barged.

Yep, I'd call it barging when you didn't wait for someone to say you could enter. My heart started racing right away. I hated it when he did that to me.

I stared at him. "What are you doing here?"

And what was he doing looking so slick in a collared shirt, dark gray with pearl buttons, while the rest of us were in jeans and T-shirts. So what if his shoulders looked broad, his hips slim, his physique imposing? It didn't mean anything. So what if the sight of him sent a sensual shiver up my spine?

"Thought I'd stop by." He stepped to one side, standing between Lachie and Nick, looking like he owned the place and maybe there was a reason for that.

I'd managed not to see him at home or in the neighborhood, and it was better that way. Yet now he seemed to think he could hold my gaze with a lingering look. Somehow he'd gotten under my skin, way under, sunk deep into my bones. I shouldn't let him have any effect at all.

No way could I forget what he'd insinuated about my drumming. Not that he'd come out and said I was crap. He hadn't needed to.

He raised his eyebrows. "You know we've got some recording coming up?"

"Of course." That came out sharper than I intended.

"I wanted to get a feel for the new dynamic. With Joel. He's new, after all."

Then it hit me that I should be nice to Morgan or the others would think I was hard to get along with. Which I wasn't. It wasn't my fault the guy brought out the worst in me.

I'd show him I could be as nice as the next person. He

might think I was stupid enough to shoot myself in the foot but I was going to prove him wrong. Very wrong.

I forced a smile. "That's an awesome idea. I'm sure Joel appreciates your presence." I stared into Morgan's chocolate brown eyes. "It's wonderful having you here. You know, someone with your expertise and experience."

He looked away. "Okay, are you all ready to get started? Because I was going to run an idea by you."

Nick nodded. "Sure."

"You've already tried out a bunch of new guys." Morgan paused. "And Holly, of course. I was thinking, maybe you should hold off on making a final decision. You can see who you like best and try them out for a couple of months first, that way you can make sure things work out."

My mouth fell open. So even if I got the gig, it wouldn't necessarily be mine? Was that what he was saying? What goddamn business was it of his anyway? My pulse raced but I held back the color spreading up my neck.

Meanwhile Nick and Lachie's brows were furrowed in thought. Minutes ago, drumming with The Merchants had been within reach whereas now my dreams were dissolving before my eyes, blown away into the distance.

Joel put his hand up. "Can I say something? When I joined the band, you didn't put *me* on probation for two months. You just said I was in."

Nick nodded. "True."

"I dunno." Lachie turned to Nick. "Maybe Morgan's right. Things are different now we're down to two original members."

Anger burned deep inside. What did Morgan have

against me? Why was he crushing my hopes, stealing the air from my lungs, the dreams at my fingertips?

I took a deep breath, struggling to hold back my temper. But when Morgan opened his mouth to speak, I couldn't help myself. I cracked the snare drum, a huge crash smashing through the air.

"Um, sorry." I sat behind my kit trying not to look guilty, taking more of those deep breaths.

Lachie laughed. Morgan didn't.

"We should probably get on with it," Nick said to him. "Take a seat, dude."

I forced myself to get my head together, no matter how crappy I felt on the inside. An idea came to me. I'd show him. In the nicest way possible.

"Actually, Morgan," I said in my sweetest voice. "I tuned my snare. Would you mind having a listen to it?" I slid off the stool, gave him my best helpless female look. "I'd really appreciate it."

As he came around, I handed him the sticks, my fingers brushing against his in a way that made my skin tingle. Damn him for making me tingle. Then he sat behind the kit and tried some rim shots first before giving the snare a good whack.

I knew exactly how this would play out. Most drummers were useless when it came to tuning and maintaining their kits. And it drove recording guys crazy because they'd spend hours tuning the drum kit and then half the day would be gone.

Meanwhile, for me, a trump card and also a show of respect for Morgan. Not that he deserved my respect. Except for his production skills which were legendary. But he'd get no respect from me for the sultry eyes and the good looks.

He glanced up from the kit. "Who'd you say tuned this?"

"I did, but you know this stuff so much better than me."

Perhaps a not-so-useless female.

He gave the snare another couple of whacks. "Nice new head. Tuned perfectly. I'm impressed." He stood. "Okay, now let's see what you can do."

Game on.

"We'll start with *Always at Midnight*." Lachie strummed the opening chords of the song, a hit from their first album, and I joined in right on cue.

When the song was over, I kept my eyes on Joel because I knew he was behind me. Couldn't bring myself to look at the others and certainly not at Morgan.

"Three more songs," Nick said.

My life depended on three more songs. The first was fast, loud, hard rock at its best. Like me. I was at my best too. For the second song, they selected a slow number so I pulled right back and chilled, kept the tempo even. They must've wanted to cover all the bases, choosing a funky song next, so I locked in with Joel on bass and channeled my inner James Brown.

Four songs, over. And I'd done good. Didn't need anyone else to tell me so. But that didn't mean I'd gotten the gig.

Joel smiled, rested his hands on the top of his bass. "Like old times, eh, Holly?"

I smiled back. So good to have him in my corner.

Nick and Lachie exchanged a long look, like two old friends who knew each other well, but I couldn't read them. Didn't dare think they liked my drumming and dreaded thinking about the alternative.

After a while, Nick said, "Holly, would you mind waiting outside for five minutes?"

"Sure." I stood, found my shaking legs could carry my weight after all.

"You too, Morgan," he added. "Hope you don't mind."

I shuffled outside, Morgan closing the door behind us. Staying under the shade of the eaves, I pressed my eyes shut as I leaned against the masonry wall that had soaked up the heat earlier in the day. Maybe it'd melt my nerves.

"You were amazing."

Did Morgan just say that? My eyes sprang open.

"You can really groove, Holly. You were swinging like an old school drummer. Like Ian Paice."

I glared at him. "Ian who?"

He stared right back. "Ian Paice from Deep Purple, classic rock drummer. You must know of him?"

I kept my mouth shut. Kept him wondering because I knew a lot more than he gave me credit for.

The silence stretched out between us while Morgan stood there, perspiration starting to stain his fancy gray shirt. You gotta love Nevada in the summer. Let him sweat.

Eventually he said, "Where'd you learn to do that?"

"YouTube."

He raked a hand through his hair, doing that cool James Dean thing again. His hair fell back into place perfectly, of course, because things always worked out for guys like him. How could he look so hunky just standing there? How could he make me feel this strange longing inside? For the band, not for him. That's what it must be.

I let him stew, then said, "I told you I'd improved since you last saw me."

"I know, I was listening."

"No, you weren't. The first time you started listening was in that rehearsal room just then."

He opened his mouth to argue, then looked away. The door opened and Joel stood there, grinning. "Come on in, guys."

Grinning. It set my nerves on edge even more because maybe he was only being polite and I'd been kidding myself and maybe I didn't groove after all. Maybe I wasn't what they wanted.

Joel held the door open while Morgan and I stepped inside, then closed it to keep the cool air in.

He was still grinning. That had to be a good sign. He looked at Lachie, then Nick.

"It'd be better coming from you guys," he said.

I stopped breathing, didn't know where to look.

Nick smiled. "Looks like The Merchants are about to take on our first female band member."

A second's silence while it sunk in. Followed by elation. I did a little dance while twirling on the spot, trying to contain myself and failing miserably. I threw my arms around Joel, jumped him, the two of us nearly falling over.

Except it wasn't Joel. I must've lost my bearings because these were Morgan's strong arms around me, his chest pressed against mine, his shoulder beneath my head. Yearning simmered low in my belly—for the band, must be for the band—the ache so deep it took my breath away.

Eventually Morgan broke off the embrace, all the guys laughing. I laughed too. I had so much to be happy about.

A new beginning, The Merchants, I couldn't believe it. My heart was racing like crazy in the best way possible.

"Thank you so much!" I screamed the words.

Nick high-fived me. "You're our new drummer. On trial. Like we said before."

I'd prove myself to them. I'd do this. No way would I blow my big chance.

I put my arm around Joel on my left and Morgan on the other side of me, and we all ended up in a group hug, energy surging through me.

Damn that Morgan—for being here, for this whole probation thing, for making me feel … something. No, nothing. I felt absolutely nothing at all.

And no way would I let any man screw things up for me again.

CHAPTER SIX

Morgan

I needed to do something mundane to get my mind off things, to switch off and wind down. Besides, I didn't want to pay a ridiculous call-out fee for someone to repair my pool filter when I could do it myself. And the mindless work was good for me.

Wolf Alice had kept me company this morning while I cleaned the grit from the filter. Full on rock 'n' roll with a girl singer and guitarist. I liked women in rock, no matter what Holly thought. And this band sounded fantastic played loud on the Megaboom speaker perched on my patio.

Holly. Better I didn't think about her captivating smile, the way she'd felt in my arms, her boobs pressed against my chest, her slender arms around my neck.

I looked down. Yep, replacing the spider gasket, that was the task at hand. I'd learned a lot about fixing stuff from my dad, which was a truckload more than I'd ever gotten from my mom. She hadn't bothered hanging around long enough for that.

Removing the nuts and bolts, I dropped them into a

red cup because it'd be a pain to lose them. I took my hat off to wipe the sweat from my brow and saw movement next door. My heart rate rose a notch.

The top of Holly's head bobbed up and down over the top of the fence while she made a couple of trips through the French doors to the patio and back again. Not that I was staring.

My gut twisted into a knot. I hadn't laid eyes on her since … since I'd made one of the biggest misjudgments of my life. Still, I didn't want to think about that, which was the whole reason for being out here in the first place.

I stood and called out, "Hello."

Back in the day, Holly had been one of the worst drummers I'd ever heard, not just bad but abysmal. How was I supposed to have known it was possible for her playing to have improved so much that she was absolutely killing it on the drums?

I sat back down with my pliers, head down as I ripped out the old spider gasket and cleaned out the foreign material from the grooves in the filter.

How could I have been such a fucking idiot? My heart sank. I'd been trying to do the right thing by Nick and Lachie, protecting them from making a bad decision with no back-out clause. A huge mistake on my part. I should've kept my big mouth shut.

Smashing noises cut through the air, loud and clear even over the top of my music. Was Holly pounding the drums on her back patio? The girl could groove and she was also pretty good with the ground and pound.

I walked to the patio and stood on one of the outdoor chairs to look over. Yep, that's exactly what she was doing.

And what was she wearing? Some sort of cropped top,

like the things women wore to the gym, with a sheer floaty dress and fitted shorts underneath. I swallowed. I should stop staring, should close my mouth, for one thing.

I called out again and waved but she didn't see me. Couldn't hear me with the headphones she had on either. Talk about loud.

Turning the volume up on my music, I trudged back to the pool and inserted the new spider gasket firmly in place. This wasn't how I'd imagined things would be, any of it. When I first saw the yard, in my head there'd been kids running around the pool. The one thing Juliet had never imagined. Not with me. Regret clawed at my stomach.

And those drums reverberated through my head. This was taking things too far. Didn't Holly care about the other neighbors? She could just as easily have played the drums inside.

Nearly finished now, I added some grease but could barely think with those drums thundering through the air. Gritting my teeth, I got up again and switched off my music completely because this was getting ridiculous.

Then I recognized the sound. The noise, to be more precise. I'd been in the business long enough that I'd know that slap back delay anywhere. Holly had stuck a microphone next to the bass drum and was putting it through a slap back delay on a P.A. system.

"Holly!" I yelled even though I knew it was useless.

Muttering under my breath, I stomped back to the pool filter. No more Wolf Alice now, only Holly's drumming, so loud it was bordering on stadium volume. Pain inched up the back of my neck, the beginnings of a headache.

All I had to do was screw the lid back on and I'd be done. She smashed the snare, a huge crash rocketing through the air. The cup with the screws slipped from my hand. The contents scattered onto the ground. While I fumed.

Right, that did it. I'd pick up the goddamn nuts and bolts later, and deal with her first. I threw my hat to the ground and stormed across to the fence, calling out and trying to get her attention. No reaction. There was only one thing to do.

I hoisted myself up, slung one leg over the fence, then the other. The drumming stopped. Holly stared. I dropped to the ground with an almighty thump.

She stood up, her eyes wide as she ripped off her headphones. "You nearly gave me a heart attack. What are you doing?"

"What do you think I'm doing?"

"Trespassing!"

Not wanting to intimidate her, I kept my distance.

I pointed to her Gretsch kit, forcing myself to speak in an even voice. "I didn't know you were a Zeppelin fan."

Hands on her hips. "I'm not."

"So what were you doing just then?"

"It's pretty obvious, isn't it?"

"Yeah, you got the most annoying song you could find and you played it over and over again through a P.A system like you're some rock star on a stage."

She shook her head, her dark curls bouncing. "I'm not a rock star."

So cute and so infuriating at the same time. I paced, first one way, then the other while she stared. But I couldn't look, or I'd end up staring at her boobs or her delicate waist or her God-only-knows-what-else.

"I won't tell you you're being a pain," I said. "You already know that."

"I wasn't bothering anyone."

"What? You were practically breaking the sound barrier." I motioned to the house on the other side. "You've got neighbors, haven't you?"

"Paul and Dennis."

"Who?"

She raised her eyebrows. "You don't know their names?" I didn't answer, and she continued. "The two lovely old guys on that side are deaf and they spend all their time at the front of their place."

"Is that so?"

"Yes, it is."

Okay, I'd barely talked to them and didn't even know their names. I got it. I was a lousy neighbor but I hadn't lived in Bedford for that long and I was busy. I'd seen them and waved, been polite, and now that wasn't enough.

"What about the people who live at the back?" I asked.

"They're out for the day."

"How do you know?"

"The kids threw their ball over the fence earlier so I talked to the mom. She told me."

Great, she'd been here all of ten minutes and already she knew everyone in the neighborhood. How did that work? How could she be edgy and endearing and strangely enigmatic all at once?

I glared at her. "You're making me look bad."

She folded her arms. "No, you're doing that all by yourself."

"Holly, I'm sorry."

That came out louder than I intended. The tendrils of the headache that'd been building shot up the back of my neck. I lifted one hand and rubbed the straining tendons on my neck.

Holly raised her eyebrows. "You're what?"

"I'm sorry for the other day at the rehearsal room. I underestimated you. Your drumming is shit hot."

"Just so we're clear on this, is that shit hot or shit?"

"Your drumming is awesome." *Like you*, the words I didn't say. "I was expecting you to play a standard four on the floor rock beat, something simple. Instead you were swinging like crazy. And you slotted in with the bass perfectly. Couldn't have been better."

Her lips curled to the hint of a smile. She stepped out from behind her kit. Drumming had given her slender muscles on her arms and shoulders, strong but slim. Good core strength too, if those tight abdominals that rippled through the sheer dress were anything to go by.

I wiped the perspiration from my brow. Nothing to do with her, and everything to do with the Nevada heat.

"Ah, I made you smile," I said.

"No, you didn't." She tried to thin her lips, then laughed it off.

"I was wrong about you, wrong about your drumming. You know all that stuff about starting over? I think we need to try for that clean slate again."

She stepped closer, made me sweat some more. "Hmm."

"I'd like to think we can be mature about this."

She rolled her eyes. "Hey, I'm way more mature than you."

I grinned, couldn't help myself when I looked at this

slender, sexy little thing trying to act all indignant. Sexy? Had that thought really entered my mind? Oh, yeah, it had.

"I like that you're not all serious and earnest," I said.

Her hazel eyes widened. "You *like* something about me?"

"There's a lot to like about you, Holly. And we're neighbors, for a while anyway, so we should try to get along"

"Well, like I told you before, I have a lot of respect for your work. I can't wait to see what you can do in the studio, that is, if The Merchants keep me as their drummer."

My stomach clenched. If she wasn't a permanent fixture in the band, that'd be because of me. Maybe I could have a word with the guys, give them my true opinion of Holly's drumming, think of other ways to help her out.

"You killed it in the audition," I said. "You're a great addition to the band and you're a lot cuter than any of the other guys."

"I'm not cute. I'm a professional."

Cute didn't begin to cover it. I swallowed, tried not to look down at her boobs in that low-necked, crop top.

"I can picture you on stage behind the drum kit with The Merchants," I said.

That brought the smile back to her face. How could I have gotten her so wrong in the first place? Maybe she had a good excuse for her drunken behavior at nineteen, for brushing me off, for not returning my calls. Especially since I'd behaved like a prick when it came to her joining the band, and I didn't have the excuse of being a teenager.

"Would you like to…" Her voice trailed off.

"To what?"

"Nothing."

It'd sounded like something but I decided not to push it. "Was my music too loud for you earlier?"

She nodded. "Yeah, I mean, I'm a fan of Wolf Alice, but it rubbed me the wrong way."

"I won't turn the music on when I'm outside."

"And I'll take the drums back into the house." She shrugged. "It's kind of hot to be playing the drums outside anyway. Even in the shade."

"I'll give you a hand."

She straightened. "I've been lugging this thing around for years. I'm not some helpless female."

I held a hand out. "I wouldn't think that for a minute. I'm just saying I'm happy to help and then maybe you can let me out the front door." I nodded toward my place. "Saves me having to jump the fence again."

She shot me a sly look. "Wouldn't want an old fellow like you to break your brittle bones."

"Exactly. Besides, I've got to go back and finish fixing the pool filter."

"That's very manly of you."

"Holly, if you need a hand with anything, you have only to let me know. I'm just next door, remember?"

She bit her lip. "There is one thing."

"Sure." I threw my hands up. "Anything."

"Jess and Lachie and maybe Nick are coming over for a drink later on this evening. You're welcome to… I mean, if you're not doing anything…"

Sounded like an invitation. Exhilaration surged through me.

"I'd love to." I grinned. "Friends?"

She nodded. "Friends."

I had a sudden urge to step closer, to cup her chin in my hands and see what happened next. I stopped myself, didn't know what was coming over me. Much safer to shake her hand, so that's what I did even though it felt pathetic.

"I'm glad we can be on good terms," I said.

If only things would stay that way. Or maybe I didn't want things to stay exactly the way they were.

I shook it off. I should get out of here, for now anyway. What the hell was I thinking?

CHAPTER SEVEN

Holly

I pulled the front door open. "Come in."

His hands full, Morgan leaned forward to kiss me on the cheek. He smelled fresh and clean. Like us. Making a new start. I kissed him back, my pulse rising at the closeness.

"I come bearing gifts." He handed me a bottle of champagne with a red bow wrapped around the neck, and looked down at his other hand. "The beers are for me."

"Thanks. You shouldn't have."

Nick and Lachie, in particular, had wanted a chance to get to know me better outside of the intensive rehearsals we'd been having, time to relax and chat, rather than concentrate on the music.

I was more than happy to have them around and wanted to make them feel as welcome as they'd made me feel. After that initial glitch at the audition, that was. The glitch that still hurt and which I ignored.

Despite everything, I wanted Morgan around too, even if I was finding it hard to admit it to myself.

"You look lovely, by the way," he said.

I touched the high neckline, the skin of my shoulders bare. "It's like a shorter version of Meghan Markle's reception dress, only I got this years ago. Back in high school. From my favorite shop."

Why did I come out with this stuff? As if Morgan would care. He might care that I hadn't bothered wearing a bra under the dress but, no, he wasn't staring. Maybe I wouldn't mind an admiring glance from him. Maybe I wouldn't mind if he tried to get a bit closer to me. A lot of things I wouldn't mind.

I motioned for him to follow me down the hall. "You know the way in. The others are on the back patio."

Morgan stopped before we reached the doorway leading to the kitchen. "I'm not late, am I?"

"No, the other guys were a bit early." Which was fine by me. Nick and Lily had arrived ahead of time so they could get home to their little boy sooner. And I'd told Jess she could come around anytime she liked. I stepped closer to Morgan, lowered my voice even though no one else would hear. "Being on time is not very rock 'n' roll."

He smiled. "No, they're not very professional like that."

"I agree. Nick and Lachie are terrible at doing the rock star thing."

Morgan's ears pricked up. "Are you playing Bruno Mars?"

"Anything wrong with that?"

He held a hand out. "Not at all, I love the production on this album. Very slick. Great sound."

I laughed. "Nick doesn't think so. He's already complained about it."

"Well, what would he know?"

"Exactly what I said." I reached for Morgan's hand, gave it a squeeze, then dropped it as soon as I realized what I was doing. "Who'd have thought we'd be agreeing on something?"

He looked down at my hand. "It's okay. You're allowed to touch me. I don't have leprosy or anything."

"Oh, good. Me neither." I nodded. "Look, I don't want you to get the wrong idea about tonight. I'm not trying to suck you into being my partner for the evening or anything."

"I didn't think that for a moment."

My heart raced at the thought he might've considered it or at my disappointment that he didn't—I wasn't sure which. Wasn't sure what was going on, only that I had to get my act together.

Unfortunately Joel and Scarlett hadn't been able to make it tonight. They were at a wedding—someone else's, not theirs. I'd already thanked Joel and told him how much it meant to me that he'd stuck up for me at the audition. Which was now ancient history now. A clean slate and all that.

I stepped into the kitchen, Morgan following close behind, and headed for my phone on the countertop.

I placed it back on the countertop. "It's run out of juice again." Typical. I was always forgetting to charge the darn thing.

Morgan's eyes widened. "What's that smell?"

"I've been baking. Told you I could cook."

I had to admit the room smelled of savory goodness. Five more minutes and the tart would be done.

Jess wandered into the kitchen, greeting us both.

"I was after some water." She reached for a glass on

the countertop. "I'll help myself."

"Yep, make yourself at home." I motioned to the dispenser on the fridge. "This place is much fancier than our old apartment."

"Sure is." She filled her glass. "We had fun, though. We always looked out for each other and you were the best roommate I ever had. Until Lachie, that is."

"Well, I'm not quite as hunky as him."

"I can help look out for you too." Morgan leaned against the oak table in the middle of the kitchen. "Now that we're neighbors. But I suspect you've done a good job taking care of yourself until now."

"Not really." I put my arm around my good friend. "Jess has done a lot for me in the past. High school wasn't exactly smooth sailing. We got bullied, both of us. Jess had to stand up for herself first and then she helped take care of me."

Morgan raised his eyebrows at Jess. "Sorry, but it's hard to imagine anyone could ever have picked on you and got away with it."

But Jess hadn't always been a bodyguard. And in high school she'd shown me how to give off an air of confidence, how not to show fear, how to retaliate. After that I'd figured out pretty quickly that bullies didn't like it when you stuck up for yourself.

Yet despite Jess, despite everything, I'd managed to get myself into a bad position after that, first of all by getting involved with a teacher and then by moving in with an abusive guy—not for long but even the shortest time was too long. The memories still took my breath away, made my heart stop for a moment.

I'd never mentioned anything about it to my mom,

though she may have suspected. It'd just be another thing I'd done wrong, another example of my ineptitude. Sometimes I didn't know who was worse, Jason or my mom, and thinking about it only sent a pang through my chest.

Lachie opened the French doors, stepping into the kitchen. "How long does it take to get a glass of water anyway?"

A welcome distraction. Lachie was always welcome as far as I was concerned.

Jess stepped across and gave him a quick kiss. "Sorry, just chatting."

He spread his arms. "And why so serious in here?"

"We're talking about getting bullied in high school," Jess said.

"Then maybe we should talk about something else."

She linked arms with him as they headed out the door. "Sure, let's go outside."

Morgan placed his hand on my lower back as he ushered me to the door, making me feel special. Maybe I didn't mind having him around so much after all.

"Oh, no, the tart." I stepped toward the oven.

"I'll give you a hand," he said. "That smells fantastic. What kind is it?"

"Caramelized onion and eggplant."

"Sounds like girl food to me. Still, it smells good."

I sliced the tart into pieces and placed them on a serving platter. "I've got this amazing kitchen so I thought I'd make the most of it."

Luckily I didn't have to start looking for a new apartment yet, but the time would come and then I'd have to downgrade.

"You can come over and use my kitchen anytime you like," he said.

Tempting. Like so many things about Morgan Masterson with his smile that switched off all my defenses and the gentle way he teased me and the strong arms I'd felt around me.

If I ignored the 'glitch' but no way could I do that when he'd nearly ruined everything for me.

My mom had reinforced this for me when I'd told her about getting into the band. *Darling, you're on probation. You know what that means.*

Yes, I did. Swallowing back the bitterness at the back of my throat, I picked up the platter.

"I'll get the door for you," he said.

We stepped out onto the patio, and I passed around the tart.

"Hey, what took you so long, Morgan?" Nick asked.

"The traffic was terrible," Morgan said.

Nick leaned back in his chair. "Did you find a parking spot?"

"Very funny. Yes, I did." Morgan leaned over to kiss Lily on the cheek. "Lovely to see you again."

He sat down beside me and, though I hadn't planned on a couples evening, that was what it felt like. Didn't seem so bad at all.

We chatted about bands and the local music scene. Nick and Lachie had some stories to tell. I still couldn't believe I was part of the band, that I was sitting at a table with them. I needed this. It wasn't as if I had a fall back position, not when the job at Charlie's hadn't eventuated. They'd only called me in to work once when someone was sick.

And soon the band would be recording. With Morgan. He'd produced The Merchants' first album, and they wanted to return to their beginnings so they could apply that same raw sound to their new songs. Except I shouldn't say 'they,' shouldn't even think it because I was part of the band too.

All I had to do was play the drums and develop a working relationship with Morgan, especially since we were due to start recording soon. Next door neighbor and record producer—that's all Morgan was.

And if I ignored the pounding in my heart, I might even believe it. But I didn't. Not for a minute.

CHAPTER EIGHT

Morgan

Girl food wasn't nearly as bad as I thought. In fact, I'd changed my mind about that completely and had been digging in to the camembert and a creamy blue cheese which went beautifully with the stuffed olives. We'd polished off the tart long ago.

I turned to Holly. "You're not a vegetarian, are you?"

"No, why do you ask?" she said.

"No reason."

And there wasn't really, except for the fact I wanted to find out everything about her.

I finished the rest of my beer. Holly had offered me some white wine earlier, thinking it'd go better with the cheese selection, but I'd assured her that everything went well with beer.

"How are the rehearsals going?" I looked to the two guys for an answer.

"Couldn't be better," Lachie said. "We started with the older stuff and moved on to the new songs pretty quickly. We're practicing the crap out of them."

"Good." I turned to Holly. "The more comfortable

you are with the songs and the guys, the better."

She nodded, didn't say anything, her expression clouding over.

Time for me to reassure her. "There's no need to stress too much about the recording side of things, Holly. We've already knocked off a few songs for the new album already so the pressure's off."

"And we've got an awesome record producer." She smiled. "In some ways, it's a bit overwhelming, the idea of recording with a band like this, because I've always been a huge fan."

"I'm a fan too."

"And in other ways, it's so familiar that it's a bit like slipping on an old, worn out coat."

I grinned. "Hey, I'm not like some old hobo's coat!"

"I'd never say you're old."

I liked it when she teased me. She had such a lovely smile, so endearing and honest. An expressive face too, especially since lately she hadn't been expressing any disdain toward me.

"Yep, now we have a new Merchant of Menace," Nick said.

Holly looked around the table. "Maybe if Jess gives me some tips I can be more menacing."

"I dunno," Nick said. "You look pretty threatening behind those drums."

"Thank you." She smiled. "I'm sure you mean that in the nicest way possible."

"You'll knock 'em dead at The Flats too," he added.

"It's just..." she began. "Well, I don't want to sound like I'm complaining, but at The Flats we'll be playing to a crowd of eighty thousand whereas I'm used to playing to crowds of eighty. The whole idea seems kind of crazy to me."

She stiffened, her shoulders scrunched, tendons in her neck straining. Maybe she'd dreamed of headlining a music festival and maybe this was also freaking her out.

It pained me to see her on edge like this so I slid my arm around her and pulled her close. I'd been dying to do this. She felt petite and strong at the same time. Felt a lot like she belonged in my arms.

"You're a brilliant drummer, Holly," I said. "You can do this."

Her hazel eyes filled with uncertainty. I let my arm drop despite the desire surging inside me. I didn't want to be too pushy, not after the rocky start we'd got off to.

"Maybe we could arrange a small gig at The Swamp," Nick said. "To get you used to being on stage with us."

"We'll take care of you." Lachie nodded. "And Cooper will be on stage at The Flats too, sharing the load for the first few songs. He won't be able to get through the whole gig so we really need you."

"I won't let you down." Holly looked at Jess, then Lily. "I'm sorry. I'm monopolizing the conversation, which is not how I planned this at all. It was supposed to be a relaxed get-together."

"Yeah, we could talk about 'me' instead." Nick spread his arms. "Holly, you'll be at the back of the stage hiding behind a drum kit. *I'm* the one everyone will be looking at."

Lachie threw a cracker at him.

Lily laughed. "How could I have married such a ham?"

Nick sidled up to her. "How could you have resisted?"

She slapped him away. "And you don't need to worry,

Holly, we're used to talking about band stuff."

"Tell me about Thomas." Holly leaned forward, her eyes lighting up. "I'd been hoping to meet him tonight."

I understood why Nick and Lily hadn't brought him along. He was a cute kid—the cutest—but the two of them could relax and have an adult conversation when he wasn't here.

Sometimes when I saw Thomas, I'd think about how that could've been me. I could've had it all, a wife, a little boy or girl, kids running around the house. God knows my house was big enough.

I swallowed the resentment in my throat but couldn't stop the anger burning in my stomach. I hadn't forgiven Juliet for that. Didn't want to forgive her.

Lily took Nick's hand into hers. "Anyway, we should get going, and relieve our babysitter."

Jess stood. "We should get going too. I've got a bit of a headache."

"Oh, no," Holly said. "I made your head hurt."

Jess smiled. "Nothing like that."

"One more thing." Holly disappeared into the kitchen while the rest of us got up and made our way through the French doors.

She handed a small box to Lily. "For Thomas."

Lily's eyes widened. "Thank you."

"It's not much," Holly said. "A Hot Wheels car. A Ferrari."

"I'd like one of those!" Lachie quipped.

I wandered back outside while Holly walked the others to the door. I should help her clean up, carry the platter and glasses back into the kitchen. And I would. But I wanted to enjoy the moment, the stillness of the air.

Holly slipped through the doors, joining me. I turned. There was a lot to enjoy around here—the smile on her face, the dark curls brushing her pretty shoulders, the white dress skimming her slender waist and the body that lay beneath.

I looked out at the garden to stop myself from staring. "Too hot during the day. Too cold at night. Still, I love living here."

"Me too." After a while, she added, "Take a seat if you like and I'll make coffee."

I turned to her. There were a lot of things I'd like, and none of them had anything to do with coffee. How could she fit so much personality into such a small package? How could I have been so wrong about her?

"You're one of the guys when it comes to the band," I said. "You know that, don't you?"

She gave a little nod, not nearly big enough for someone who was such a powerhouse on the drums.

I held her gaze. "Your drumming, your work ethic, the way you practice all the time, your attitude. You're the whole nine yards."

"Yep, I've got a great attitude."

The way she nodded so enthusiastically, a smile creeping to her lips, made me laugh.

"What?" She spread her arms. "I was agreeing."

"You're right." I could've stared into her pretty hazel eyes all night. "You're not the same girl you were four years ago, and it was unfair of me to think that."

Her face clouded over. Had I said the wrong thing? I was trying to apologize.

"What is it, Holly?"

She stepped back. "I'm surprised you'd bring that up."

"Bring what up?" We had to get this out in the open, one way or another. "Maybe we both need to sit down."

She perched on the edge of a chair. "Okay."

I sat beside her. "Look, after that night, I thought you must've hated me. I called and sent texts. I even left a message with one of the guys in your old band. But you didn't return my calls. What was I supposed to think?"

She held my gaze, a frown forming. "You really want to know why I didn't return your calls? At first, I thought you were a nice guy, taking care of me."

"I was."

She'd been shit-faced drunk, barely able to stand, and two guys had insisted they'd take her home, but all they wanted was to take turns with her. Of that, I'd had no doubt. I'd even had to punch one of the guys to get him off her. Then I'd taken her home to make sure she was safe.

Her eyes hardened. "Then, I thought something else."

"What? What did you think? I didn't trust those two other dudes. I couldn't have lived with myself if some bad shit happened to you and I'd simply stood by."

"I was in a bad way. Legless."

"You couldn't even get your key in the front door so I unlocked it for you, then took you to your room so you didn't fall asleep in the hallway. You pulled back the covers and sat up in bed. I took off your shoes and went to get a glass of water. For *you*, not me. I didn't need the water. When I got back, you were lying in bed, so I left."

"When you got back… "

"Yeah, that's what I said."

Holly, lying in bed naked with the covers barely covering her, her skin so pale, her breasts bare, a picture that'd been permanently imprinted on my memory. I'd pulled the covers up ever so gently, making sure I didn't touch her, no matter how much I may have wanted to. Because that wouldn't have been right.

Realization dawned.

My mouth fell open. "You think I took your clothes off?"

She nodded.

"Surely you don't think…?" I stared. "I would never… No, you couldn't possibly have thought I'd take advantage of a woman in that position."

Her lips thinned. "When I first woke up, I panicked and thought the worst, then got my act together." She held a hand out. "So, no, I don't think that you and I… I didn't think that happened. But I was naked. I thought you'd undressed me."

In my dreams maybe.

I told her, "Far as I know, *you* took your clothes off, because there was no one else around and it sure as hell wasn't me. For the record, I covered you up before I left."

I let that sink in.

"I'm sorry." Her expression grew pained. "Sorry I got so drunk, sorry I put you in that position, and sorry I assumed you'd taken my clothes off."

"You believe me?"

"Of course I do. But I was nineteen back then."

"It's okay." I slipped my hand onto her knee, hoping my touch would be welcome. "I was nineteen once too. I've done my share of dumb shit."

"I'm glad."

"Glad I've done a lot of stupid crap?"

"No, glad it sounds like you're forgiving me."

"I'm actually not a very forgiving person, but this is different."

She lowered her gaze, and I thought about taking my hand away, truly I did, but I waited. Reaching across, she took my hand into both of hers. Relief coursed through me. The other emotion coursing through me had nothing to do with relief and everything to do with lust. I took a long, slow breath.

She let my hand go, then said, "Sorry."

"Don't be."

I forced myself to hold back the growing need in my groin. Though Holly was a powerhouse on the drums, she was more delicate than she appeared, maybe even damaged. And no way would I hurt her, not even accidentally.

"Look, I should probably get going," I said. "Walk me to the door and we'll call it even."

She brightened. "Deal."

I tried to make the trip to the front door take as long as possible. Maybe I should've taken her up on that offer of coffee. Was it too late to backtrack? Probably.

But I couldn't argue with my gut. It was time to go.

I stopped inside the door while she pulled it open.

"Holly, I'm glad we cleared that up."

She looked up at me, her eyes wide. "So am I."

I placed my hands on her shoulders, felt the little muscles beneath her bare skin. I wanted to pull her closer, wanted to take her into my arms, wanted to do a lot of things. I did none of them. I let my hands drop.

Her lips curved to a smile as she stood on tiptoe, sliding her hands onto my jaw to pull my face closer. She pressed her lips against mine, so soft, so gentle. Wow, she was full of surprises.

We stood staring into each other's eyes. Then she said, "You're allowed to kiss me, you know."

"Isn't that what we just did?"

"No," she said softly. "This is a kiss."

She snaked her arms around my neck, her fingers intertwined in my hair as she drew me closer. I slid my hands onto her slender waist, wrapping my arms around her. Her mouth came crashing up onto mine, and this time there was no doubt. *This was a kiss*. She tasted like white wine and felt like everything I'd ever wanted.

Eventually we broke off the kiss.

"Goodnight, Morgan."

She closed the door behind me. So what the hell was I supposed to think after that? What was this woman doing to me?

CHAPTER NINE

Holly

I'd proven myself during rehearsal sessions with The Merchants but recording was a different bag all together. I hadn't let on that I'd never even been in a recording studio before. Didn't want to look like a complete beginner and certainly didn't want the guys second-guessing their decision to take me on.

An assortment of rugs covered the polished oak floorboards and a couple had been thrown over an amp stack. For sound absorption or maybe for an artful look, I wasn't sure which. No windows. We didn't need them with the standard lamps that made for a soft glow in the room. Moody and atmospheric, that was how I'd describe it, probably to encourage creativity. If only I was feeling creative.

Joel took off his bass, along with his headphones. "Take five, guys. I just want to stretch my legs."

"But you're standing," Nick said. "Aren't they already stretched?"

They were all on their feet while I sat behind the drums. Or cowered.

"Sure thing." Morgan's voice came through loud and clear over the headphones.

I glanced at him through the window into the control room, didn't dare stare. None of this was his fault. The poor guy was only doing his job. It was pretty obvious where the problem lay. With me.

Joel wandered closer and said in a low voice, "You gotta relax."

I nodded, tried to swallow back my nerves. I took off the cans, got out from behind the drums, and walked around.

Ginger got up from where she'd been crouched in a corner. "I'm getting a little stiff."

It should've been weird having Cooper's girlfriend in the studio with us. Instead the guys liked having her here and so did I, even if most of the time I completely forgot about her.

She was putting together a book about rock 'n' roll in Frankston, and today's recording session was part of the band's story. Cooper was having a bad day. Otherwise he'd have dropped by to see how things were going.

Band manager, Brett, was missing too. Out of town. Just as well so he couldn't see me screwing this up.

My mother's words rang through my head. *There are lots of good drummers around. I hope they don't get rid of you.* Nerves rattled around inside me. I'd invited my parents over for a barbecue in a few days, my anxiety increasing at the thought.

Morgan pulled open the door to the studio, leaning in the doorway, looking effortlessly handsome and masculine.

I'd kissed him the other night. I'd more than kissed him. I'd reveled in it. And I'd want to kiss him again if I didn't want to kill him right now.

Lachie held his hand out for a knuckle bump. "Hey, man."

I sat back down behind the kit. "It's the click track. It's throwing me."

"A necessary evil," Morgan said. "Most people don't like them."

The click track was a lot like a metronome, a click-click audio cue that came in through the headphones while we were recording to make sure the band kept in time. Or me. To make sure *I* kept in time.

Morgan insisted on using a click so he'd be able to blend different takes later on to get the best possible result. I knew all this. And it made no difference. I still didn't see why we couldn't try this without the click. As if the damn click track was a matter of life and death, and we had to do this Morgan's way.

"I've got an idea," he said. "How about if we sample the high hat and use that for the click track? Then the sound isn't just an annoying click."

I had nothing to lose. "Sure."

"It'll only take five minutes." Morgan left the room.

Seconds later, I heard his instructions through the headphones, then hit the high hat just once.

After a while, he said, "Listen to this. It should make for a smoother sound."

He played the new click that used the high hat. The other guys nodded.

"Okay, another take," Morgan said. "When you're ready."

We played the song again, a new number Nick and Lachie had written together, a great song. The song wasn't the problem.

We did it again and again. The repetition didn't bother me. That was all part of the process. Problem was, I didn't seem to be getting any better. It felt like I was wearing someone else's clothes, as if my mother had dressed me, because I didn't feel like myself at all.

After a while, Nick said, "Why don't we break for lunch?"

Lachie placed his guitar on a stand behind him. "Yeah, I'm starving."

Which seemed to be the general consensus. Morgan wandered back into the studio and a discussion about burgers versus Chinese followed. Morgan… Better I didn't think about him.

"Are you coming?" Joel asked.

"No, I brought some food with me."

Knowing I'd need a snack, I'd stopped at a French bakery on the way for a croissant.

"Can I bring back anything for you?" Joel asked.

I nodded. "Just a mineral water."

"What about you, Ginger?" he asked.

She shook her head. "I told Cooper I'd only be a couple of hours, so I should get going."

Yep, a couple of hours I'd wasted, time out of my day and theirs. I took a deep breath, tried to shake off my trepidation.

A lot of kissing of cheeks went on, as the guys thanked Ginger for being there, then left, clearly driven by their stomachs.

She slung her camera bag over her shoulder. "Thanks for letting me take photos today."

I shrugged. It was nothing. Today had been a great big nothing.

"You can tell Cooper how much the guys miss his drumming," I said.

She stopped by the door, took a moment. "He misses it too."

A pang shot through my heart. I could still play drums. I could go for it day and night if I wanted to. Whereas Cooper … it didn't bear thinking about.

"I'm sorry," I called out, but she'd already left.

Despite the guilt that flooded me, I managed to eat my croissant without choking. I still had to eat, after all. Besides, the silence in the room gave me some solace, the crunching of my croissant deadened by the rugs, soft furnishings, and acoustic panels in the ceiling.

I rummaged around in my bag for some hand sanitizer, then stepped over to Nick's two guitars resting on stands next to his amp. Nick had always longed for a signature guitar and he was finally getting one, a Gibson ES-335 Semi Hollow that'd be ready in time for The Flats.

My fingers hovered over the acoustic. Should I? He wouldn't mind. I took the guitar over to a nearby chair, my back to the control room. I strummed a few chords. Not so bad.

I started playing and it all came back to me, the tunes I used to write. Not proper songs, not anything that'd compare with The Merchants, but songs that were mine.

When I first saw you
Cross the street
Well I was spellbound
Swept off my feet

I kept strumming, singing, and the rest of the room disappeared.

Well you are always
In my dreams
I hear you laughin'
Or so it seems
I don't know fortune, don't know fame
And I don't even know your name

The song over, I rested my hand on top of the guitar. Seconds later, the studio door opened. Morgan stood there, his eyes wide.

He closed the door behind him. "That was beautiful."

A wave of fresh nerves flooded me. Nerves and something else. Desire, maybe. He must've been in the control room where he could hear me through the microphones in the room but I hadn't known he was still there.

"Um, thanks."

"I didn't know you could sing, not like that anyway. You've really got your own thing happening with the vocals." He paused. "How do you do it, Holly?"

"Do what?"

He pulled a chair close to mine. "How can you be such a stressed-out mess on the drums and now you're like Taylor Swift on the guitar? That's not even your instrument."

"I'm not like Tay Tay. Not famous, not talented, not successful."

"Taylor is all of those things. I'd never knock her or her music. But you're real, Holly. You're honest. You don't hide your feelings. What you see is what you get." He threw his hands up. "I just don't know what's going on today with your drumming."

I thought the worst. I tried not to, but I did.

"If I don't get my shit together, they'll ditch me, won't they?"

Morgan shook his head. "No, that's not how they work. You're one of the guys now. Don't forget it."

"Actually, I'm not in the band yet. I'm on probation."

Not that I blamed Morgan for that anymore. Given my performance today, it only seemed sensible that they'd taken me on a trial basis.

Morgan still seemed to get in the way, though, like with the click track. Or with the way his lingering look distracted me, made me melt on the inside, made me feel something I shouldn't.

He held my gaze. "Look, if you can nail this, there's no way they'd get rid of you. You fit with them. This feels right." He took my hand into his. "Can't you feel it, Holly?"

The warmth of his touch seeped into my fingers, along with a sense of comfort almost like a homecoming. Almost like I belonged … with him.

"I feel like I'm on the edge of something big." Was I talking about Morgan? Or the band?

"You should do what I do, and trust your gut."

"How do you do that?"

I'd grown up being told nearly everything I did was wrong. Later, I'd made some terrible decisions, particularly where men were concerned. How could I trust my gut when my judgment was so skewed?

He held my gaze. "You can do this, Holly. Don't

doubt it for a minute."

"Okay, you think I should go with my gut?"

He nodded.

"Then that's what I'll do. When the other guys get here, I'll be like a new woman."

Morgan smiled. "I kind of like the old one."

My heart softened and then, as if on cue, the door burst open. The others came charging in, Joel ahead of the other two, a bottle of San Pellegrino in his hand.

"Here you go." He handed me the bottle.

It didn't take long before we were back in place, ready for the next track with Morgan in the control room.

I tapped the high hat, got their attention. "Okay, guys, I've got an idea. Let's try the song *without* the click track to see if we can make this work."

"Okay," Nick said.

I looked at Morgan in the control room, his lips thin, jaw tight.

"We *need* the click." He leaned forward into the mic. "It's integral to the recording process."

I held my ground. "Let's try it. That's all I'm saying."

The other guys mumbled their agreement, which was as much as I needed.

As soon as I started drumming, the song felt different, felt right. And I let it rip, slowing down during the quiet parts of the song and playing a fraction ahead of the beat during the fast bits.

The song finished. Silence. I looked around the room.

Nick grinned. "That was fucking amazing."

I let out a sigh, my shoulders relaxing, a smile creeping to my lips. "One more time."

We played the song a few more times, each take a little

more dynamic than the last. The song had movement. Hell, we rocked. That's what this was all about.

"I think we've got it." Morgan's voice heard through the headphones. "While we're on a roll, let's get onto the next number."

Yep, it was onto the next song. No resting on my laurels for me. We played one of Joel's songs, maybe the best song he'd ever written. *A Beating Heart* captured his feelings about new love and the fear of breaking up before you'd even started.

Nick swept his arm toward me. "We have it again. Fucking amazing."

Joel and Lachie nodded in agreement. This time the smile on my face was a full blown grin. I looked through the window at Morgan, also grinning.

We did a few more takes, not too many, not enough to suck the energy from the performance, then we all gathered in the control room to listen to the recordings.

I stood close to Morgan, or maybe it was the other way around, while the other three lounged on the leather sofa. A lot like being in someone's living room, only with a huge console, racks of pre-amps, and an extremely sophisticated sound system.

We basked in our glory, an amazing feeling, a wonderful way to end the day.

Lachie's lips thinned. "I screwed up that guitar riff."

"No way," Nick said. "No one's going to notice. You were on fire. That third take is awesome."

Followed by some more basking. Morgan and I stayed in the control room while the other guys packed up their guitars and Joel his bass. My Gretsch kit and the amps were staying set up because we'd be back again tomorrow.

The guys waved as they left.

Morgan dropped down onto the sofa beside me. "A shaky start but you were crazy good today."

I couldn't stop smiling. "Thanks."

He slid closer, our thighs touching. "What was with you pulling your weight when it came to ditching the click track?"

"I was following my gut." My pulse quickened. "Like I am now."

Leaning across, I pressed my lips against his. Not lightly. *Gentle* was the last thing I wanted. Desire simmered deep in my belly, my lips tingling. Screw *gentle*.

I cupped his chin in my hands, drew him closer, and kissed him the way I wanted to, long and hard. Kissed him like my life depended on it. Because maybe it did.

We had to come up for air eventually. He looked good enough to eat and I wanted to devour him.

"Come back to my place." I squeezed his hand. "I'll cook."

My hand still in his, he stood up. "Sounds good. Because I'm hungry."

So was I. Hungrier than I'd been in a long time.

CHAPTER TEN

Morgan

Normally I wouldn't have left the studio until late, not with a day's demo tapes to go through and my head buzzing with ideas.

Normal just went out the window. I'd tidied up a few things at the studio, then stopped at home for a quick shower and to pick up a bottle of wine and a few beers. Also because Holly had told me to give her time to get organized.

By the looks of it, *organized* meant she'd stopped at the store, had a shower, and got changed, her hair still damp along the hairline. She'd let it down tonight, her dark curls going a little wild while she stood with her back to me facing the kitchen bench.

I sidled up behind her, placed my hands on her hips. "Anything I can do?"

She held up the meat mallet in her hand. "I've got it under control."

I pulled her hair behind her neck, pressing a little kiss onto the bare skin. Her back arched. I liked getting a response, liked a lot of things about where this was headed.

She turned to me. "I hope you're not going to argue with a woman who's got a hammer in her hand."

"Maybe I'd best leave you to it."

"Exactly."

Never before had a woman looked so sexy tenderizing a hunk of meat, her waist tightening, hips shifting beneath the fabric of her red dress. Was she even wearing a bra under that thing? I swallowed. I could get used to this.

She tossed the sirloins onto a hot skillet. "I got steak because it's quick and I haven't exactly had hours to prepare the meal. Also in case you were still worried I was a vegetarian!"

"Nope, not worried."

Not even close.

"Why don't you pour the wine?" she said.

Minutes later, the steaks were ready, the salad tossed— I took care of that—and oven roasted asparagus served at the table.

She sipped her wine. "You'll have to eat all your greens."

I swallowed a mouthful of vegetables. "You weren't kidding when you said you were a good cook. You're good at a lot of things."

She gave me a shy smile that told me she didn't believe me.

"You're a damn good drummer for one thing," I added.

She brightened. "Thanks."

"Like today. The main reason I wanted to record with a click was because with Cooper, it was the only way to keep him in line. He's a brilliant drummer—don't get me wrong—only with a very different style, whereas you work more by feel."

"My drumming's not perfect." She shrugged. "But maybe it's the imperfections that can make a song sound so good."

"Well, it worked. The sound for those songs was so much more human." A pang of guilt shot through me. "I'm not perfect either. If I was, maybe I'd have known we should ditch the click track from the start."

"You're not to blame, and I can tell the guys love working with you."

I raised my eyebrows. "And you?"

She smiled. "So far, so good."

The recording process wasn't about me. It was about the band and bringing out their vision. Having Holly on board had changed things for the band. For me too.

She peered over the top of her wine glass. "I feel lucky to have gotten where I am. I certainly never thought of drumming as a career when I started. Never really had a plan. It's all hit and miss with me. I've done so many dumb things you wouldn't believe it."

"I wouldn't hold any of that against you."

"You might if you knew." She served herself some more asparagus. "I had an affair with a teacher once. I'd say that was pretty dumb."

What? Wine spluttered as I lifted the glass to my mouth, then wiped my chin.

"See," she said. "Told you so."

"You had sex with a teacher?"

"No. Yes. Kind of." She looked down, then up again. "I was eighteen so it wasn't as if I was underage or anything."

Still, it sounded creepy. A teacher. I tried to imagine it, a young Holly and a more mature man, someone who shouldn't have had his hands on her in the first place. My chest heaved, anger burning in my gut. I'd punched guys out for less than that.

"It was definitely consensual," she added. "School had just finished and I should have known better."

"Maybe *he* was the one who should have known better."

She shrugged. "Back then, it was Jess to the rescue again, giving me advice, helping me pick up the pieces. Turned out it was pretty easy to break off with him."

I reached across the table for her hand. "Sounds to me like you got taken advantage of."

As much as I hated to admit it, I could imagine exactly how she'd drive a man wild with desire without even trying. Hell, I didn't have to do a lot of imagining for that. It was no excuse, though. Men were born with a brain as well as a dick. And a heart. Maybe that guy should've been using it.

"Doesn't mean you were dumb," I said. "Just young."

"Then I must've stayed young for a long time." Her eyes narrowed, filling with pain. "I've done stranger shit than that."

"Everyone makes mistakes, Holly."

"It's not just that. Somehow I always seemed to attract assholes."

I damned well hoped not. "Really?"

"Not you!" She leaned forward, squeezed my hand. "I didn't mean you were an asshole."

It was worth the insult to get her attention. I didn't

know what else she'd been through, but we could discuss it another time. She didn't seem quite ready to talk anyway, and talking wasn't foremost on my mind.

"You should eat." I nodded toward her plate. "I'd have thought you might be one of those fashionably-late types, but you seemed to want to eat early tonight. You must've been hungry."

"Oh, you know." Her foot rubbed up against my leg under the table. "I thought if we ate early, we'd have more free time … for later on."

Blood rushed through my body. I shoveled down the rest of my dinner in record time, washing it down with a couple of mouthfuls of red wine and wondering why it was taking her so long to finish her meal.

She sliced a piece of steak, paused before putting it in her mouth. "Have you always lived in Frankston?"

"Yeah."

"What about your family? Your upbringing?"

"Oh, just the usual."

She swallowed a mouthful, then raised her eyebrows. "Well, aren't you Mr. Talkative."

"Okay." I figured I could talk and she could eat and that'd work for both of us. "There's my older brother, Scott. My folks divorced when I was twelve. By the time I was fourteen, Mom remarried and moved to Florida. For the weather, she said. As if it was freezing cold in Nevada."

I didn't bother to hide the resentment in my voice. Couldn't if I tried.

Compassion glimmered in Holly's eyes. "She left you and your brother?"

"She was never there for us anyway. I was close to

Scott when I was little. Not so much anymore. He moved away years ago. He's a stockbroker."

Scott was a lot like Mom, distant in every way that mattered. Some time during my teenage years, it'd stopped feeling like a family, and that wasn't simply down to my parents' divorce.

It'd be good to have one of those one day—a family, people to love who loved me back, children of my own. None of that seemed boring to me. Scott had kids and it seemed to have worked for him. God knows I loved my two nephews but it wasn't the same as having your own.

"And your dad?" Holly asked.

I pointed to her plate. "You need to keep eating."

She smiled, picked up a large forkful of salad. "Now you're turning into Mr. Slave Driver."

"My old man is my number one fan. We never had much money growing up, but he never let that stand in his way. He's turned into a bit of a hermit now. Lives out past Fort Greenly. I should visit him soon, but it's quite a drive."

Her eyes widened. "I'd love to come!"

I laughed. "I didn't ask."

"You didn't need to. Besides, I'll be good company, I promise. And I've kind of got an ulterior motive."

"What does 'kind of' mean?"

She put down her knife and fork, hesitated for a moment. "My parents are coming around in a few days for a barbecue and I wanted to invite you over. Not so much to meet them, as for moral support. I don't always get along with my mom. She's a bit odd sometimes."

More time with Holly was definitely no skin off my nose. "Sure, I can do that."

She stood, reaching across for my empty plate. "Good, that's decided then."

Taking her to meet my dad seemed kind of weird when we weren't properly dating, hadn't even had sex yet. That could change …very quickly.

Besides, what the hell? I'd love to show her off to my dad.

I picked up the empty salad bowl and vegetable platter. "I'll help you clean up."

She turned from the bench. "But you're the guest. You should sit down while I make coffee."

I placed the bowl in the sink, sliding one hand onto her delicate waist. "I don't want coffee, Holly. I want you."

She covered my hand with hers, grabbed it, pulling it up onto her breast, and I could have exploded right there and then. No bra. Not much between me and her. Soft and firm and seductive. Man, I wasn't wrong about wanting her.

I pulled her close, wrapping my arms around her as I covered her mouth with mine. She tasted like red wine and felt petite pressed up against me.

She took control, jammed me against the bench, her slender body molding against mine as she pulled my head down for another kiss. Mouths open, tongues rolling, I couldn't get enough of her.

Damn it, I could've swept the remaining dishes from the table, taken her there and then in the kitchen, put the oak table to good use. But that wouldn't have been proper, not for our first time. I wanted to do this right.

She undid the buttons of my shirt, sliding one hand onto my chest while the other pulled at my butt. I wanted her little hands all over me. Needed her. I lifted the hem of her dress higher, my fingers wandering over her hips while she fumbled with the button of my jeans.

All of a sudden, she pushed me away, looking up at me through the loose curls that fell over her face.

"The bedroom," she said.

She motioned for me to follow her out of the kitchen down the hallway. I let her lead the way, admiring the sway of her hips. She slowed in the middle of the hall, reaching for the zipper behind her and slipping out of the dress. Her sandals too. She curled her index finger for me to follow, and I caught a glimpse of her magnificent bare boob. Hell, I'd follow her into a pit of snakes to get a better look.

Ripping off my shirt, I followed, tossed the damn thing in the hall. I stood in the doorway while Holly prowled across the bed to switch on the bedside light, bathing the room in a soft glow. She lay across the bed, resting on her elbows, beckoning me with her eyes.

I kicked off my shoes, jeans, and briefs in record time, grabbing a condom from my pocket in the process. Leaning over the bed, I hooked my fingers over her panties. She lifted her butt so I could slide them off.

Why hadn't I got her naked sooner? Why had I wasted so much time?

The first time was fast and urgent. I needed it. We both did. After that we took our time, rolling around on the bed, exploring each other's bodies, touching, tasting, feeling. Maybe even a bit of talking, not too much.

Somewhere along the line we both got thirsty so Holly went to the kitchen to bring back two beers. A naked woman with beer. Life didn't get much better than this.

Or did it? Despite the satisfaction simmering in my

stomach, something niggled at me, a yearning for something more.

I liked having Holly around, wanted to be with her. How wonderful if things could stay this way, if I could depend on her, if she could be there for me. Because I'd love to be there for her.

If only this could last.

CHAPTER ELEVEN

Holly

Though not in the middle of nowhere, Morgan's dad's house wasn't far from it. Fort Greenly was a fifteen minute drive away from his place but the only thing between the two was a gas station and a lot of road. And I was hardly exaggerating.

Yet somehow his dad's place wasn't the way Morgan had described it. A wicker chair and small table sat on the porch overlooking a garden with a couple of trees and various cacti and drought resistant plants nestled in elegant rockeries. Not fancy. It didn't need to be. Like the house itself.

Morgan's father had shoved glasses of iced water into our hands as soon as we'd arrived. Now he poured tea from a pot while we sat on the living room sofa with Johnny Cash playing in the background.

Pete handed me a cup. "Here you go. Sometimes tea is the most refreshing thing to have in the heat."

I took the cup. "Thank you. Is it okay if I help myself to a muffin?"

"Why sure. You made them." He chuckled. "I think

you're entitled to have one."

"They freeze very well, by the way. The muffins, that is."

I took a bite of orange and poppy seed goodness.

Pete turned to Morgan who was already digging in. "You'd better watch your waistline if you keep getting fed like this."

Morgan swallowed. "Holly's a good cook, all right."

His father looked like he took care of himself. He was still strong and lean, if a little shorter than Morgan, and the lines on his face suited him. He leaned over to pat the Labrador at his feet, Dolly, named after one of his favorite singers.

I sipped my tea, and found it quenched my thirst better than the water had. A few family photos sat on the sideboard, and I couldn't resist so I got up while Morgan and his dad chatted.

I picked up one of the pictures. "This must be you and your brother?"

"Yeah, I'm the handsome one," he said.

"Sure are."

He looked about fourteen or fifteen in the photo, like a skinnier younger version of the guy in front of me now. Hardly surprising. Meanwhile his brother was scowling, looking decidedly pissed off.

"And who's this?" I couldn't keep the teasing smile from my face as I pointed to a photo of Pete standing in front of a small room with a microphone hanging up behind a window.

"That was ten years ago," Pete said.

"Well, you haven't changed a bit." I turned to Morgan. "What was this place?"

"That's the old studio, before I built the extension. It's still there if you want to take a look."

I did. "And what's this? Is that a vocal booth?"

We hadn't used the booth in the new studio for our recent recording because music from the other band instruments weren't leaking into the vocal mic.

"Yep, Dad made that for me," Morgan said. "He downloaded plans, built the timber structure, lined it with acoustic material, installed the window, built the whole thing."

"Wow."

"I didn't have a lot of money back then. Dad helped. A lot. And not just with the vocal booth. I couldn't have done it without him."

"It was the least I could do," Pete piped up. "I always knew Morgan's studio was going to be a success."

I did the math. "So, Morgan, you were twenty when you started up on your own?"

He grinned. "Yep, luckily I didn't know how young I was, and no one told me it couldn't be done!"

So different from my life where I'd grown up being told I wasn't good enough or talented enough or *anything* enough. Better I didn't think about that now. It'd only drag me down.

"What about Scott?" I asked. "Where does he live?"

"Chicago." Pete nodded. "I stayed with him for a week last year because he's way too busy to visit. It was my only chance to see my grandkids." His face lit up. "They're four and six."

I sat down, whacked Morgan gently on the shoulder. "You never mentioned them."

"Probably because I don't get to see them nearly

enough." He turned to his father. "Scott's the same with me too. Won't visit. He's left Frankston way behind. I wouldn't be surprised if he's taken it off his birth certificate."

I looked at Pete. "This isn't at all how I'd imagined it. I thought you were a bit of a hermit."

He straightened. "I'm not a hermit. Who the hell said I was a hermit?"

"Dad." Morgan gave him a serious look. "Come on. You live out here in the middle of nowhere. You hardly leave the house unless you have to."

"I go to work five days a week."

"Yes, because you have to," Morgan said. "You'd much rather stay here with Dolly."

"That's because she's better company than most people." He leaned over and rubbed the dog's neck. "I'm never on my own with Dolly and I'm never going to turn into a damn hermit or stop working. I've got plans. If they think I'm too old to be a landscaper at that school, I'm going to start up my own handyman business. You're never too old."

Nope, with the Mastersons, it seemed you could never be too young or too old. What a wonderful way to live.

I sipped my tea, looked at his father. "I imagined you might be a grumpy, old man."

He laughed. "Ha! You got that part right."

"But you're not. You're funny."

"No, I'm not." Pete couldn't keep the smile from his face. "You had any good country musicians come by the studio, son?"

Morgan shook his head. "No such thing. You just used 'good' and 'country' in the same sentence."

Pete leaned back in his chair. "Finest music there is. Better than hip-hop and that rap crap that young people listen to."

"Who are your favorites?" I asked.

"The greats, Waylon Jennings, Willie Nelson, Tammy Wynette, maybe even Dixie Chicks, and that Shania is still a mighty fine woman. I'm not a fan of that new country music that's all about a girl and a truck and getting some brews." He waved it off.

"We always had music playing when I was growing up," Morgan said. "If you call 'country' music."

Pete tried to look stern, then cracked up. After they'd talked and we'd had a second pot of tea, we rose to leave. Pete picked up one of the photos I'd been looking at earlier.

"I'm proud of both of my sons." He put the picture back down on the sideboard. "What kind of father would I be if I wasn't?"

Tears burned at the back of my eyes, hot and sudden. I held them back, wondering where the hell they'd come from because I didn't usually let things get to me like this.

Morgan pulled his father into a big hug, his eyes closed, holding him close. Something in Morgan's smile made me think maybe he was holding back some tears too.

Pete broke off the embrace and pulled open the front door. "You heard from your mother?"

"The usual." Morgan shrugged. "I call her every few weeks and she's happy to talk but never quite finds the time to phone me herself."

"It's good you keep in touch, son." He grinned. "Wouldn't want you to turn into a hermit, like me."

"No need to get sarcastic in your old age." Morgan

waved goodbye. "There's heaps of room at my place whenever you want to come over."

"Sure thing." Pete shook my hand. "Lovely meeting you."

Morgan and I had two hours on country roads ahead of us in the Range Rover. The leather seat felt good against the bare skin of my legs, if a little warm. Meanwhile the air conditioning blasted into my face as the car took off, such a relief. I loved my Honda Fit but I could get used to this sort of luxury.

I cleared my throat. "Your dad's a funny guy."

"So you said."

"I'm sorry about your mom and how things worked out between the two of you."

Morgan concentrated on the road ahead of him. "The way I see it, they worked out just the way she planned."

I heard the hurt in his voice, felt his pain. I had plenty of issues with my mom but she'd never left me, and she'd been there through my teenage years even if she hadn't provided much in the way of support.

"I don't know what would drive a woman to leave her kids," I said. "I mean, when you have children, they're your whole reason for living."

Silence, the uncomfortable kind, the sort that made my gut clench. I'd hurt him, the last thing I wanted to do.

After a while I said, "I'm sorry. That was out of line."

"No," he said. "You nailed it."

"Still, it's not my place."

"You don't know how true your words were. It's not just my mom. It's something else. Someone."

"I'll start at the beginning. With Naomi. She didn't believe in me the way my dad did when I was first starting out, so she dumped me to look for someone with more money and better prospects."

I couldn't understand the way some people's minds worked. "Whoa, money's not everything."

He shrugged. "We were both young. Then there's Juliet. We weren't quite that young. We lived together for four years, broke up when I was twenty-six. Twenty-six going on a hundred. I thought she was the one but it turned out she didn't think so much of me."

"Maybe she got that bit wrong."

"She was wrong about a lot of things. One big thing came between us. She got pregnant and didn't tell me."

My mouth fell open, a pang cutting through my chest.

"Turns out she didn't want to be a mom. Didn't want to be with me. A lot of things she didn't want." He paused. "She got rid of the baby, and broke off with me."

He stared ahead at the open road, trying to hide the pain in his eyes, but how could he when I felt it too?

"Oh, Morgan..."

"I'm not saying I was ready to be a father at twenty-six either but I reckon I would've smartened up fast. I kept having flashbacks after that, visions of Juliet at the clinic, me rushing in in time to stop her, visions of a baby being born, visions of this stuff when I hadn't even been there." He glanced at me, then back at the road, took a few moments. "I had nightmares. Used to wake up in a cold sweat. It wasn't right. Shouldn't have happened that way."

"I'm so sorry, Morgan."

Tears welled in my eyes at his loss because this had been a great loss for Morgan. And I wasn't sure he was over it. Must've been hard for his ex too.

I squeezed his thigh, then pulled my hand back. "I

don't know what to say. I'm pleased you opened up to me. I won't tell anyone about this."

"I didn't think you would."

After a while, I asked, "Have you had any girlfriends since then?"

"A few." He smiled wanly, glancing across at me. "The only girlfriend who matters to me is you."

I couldn't help but smile. "So I'm your girlfriend now, am I?"

He smiled too. Kept driving.

Maybe he trusted me just a little. We'd come so far, the two of us. How warm that made me feel, despite the sinking in my stomach about what he'd just told me.

I stared at the passing countryside, flat and scrubby, a huge blue sky above us. Sometimes you didn't have to look far to see hope. I swallowed, my throat tight. I had my own secrets too. We all did. And I was too ashamed to talk about mine, about Jason, the biggest mistake of all.

The first time, it'd been a shove. I'd ignored it, thought it was a mistake on Jason's part, told myself there was no reason for me to feel like shit. Then he shoved me again. After that, it'd been a slap so hard that it knocked me backward. I didn't wait around to see what would happen the next time. My stomach still knotted in fear at what I'd been through.

I glanced at Morgan, then shifted my gaze back to the wide open road ahead that should have made it a little easier for me to talk, but didn't. Another time perhaps. I should lighten things up.

"Families, eh," I said. "Who needs 'em?"

Morgan had been let down too. I wasn't the only one. Besides, my life was looking up with him in it, not to mention The Merchants. I already had more good things in my life than I deserved.

Maybe Morgan could be there for me. Maybe things would work out this time. Maybe...

It didn't mean this was love. What was the big deal about love anyway?

CHAPTER TWELVE

Morgan

Holly pressed a quick kiss to my lips, then pulled me inside her front door. "I'm so glad you're here. I'm having a barbecue crisis. Can't work the damn thing and I can't let on or I'm going to look like a complete idiot."

"Of course I can help."

"I need you. Can you pretend you're in charge of the barbecue, like it's your baby and you don't want me going near it?"

"Sure."

"Honestly, if you can fix a pool filter, I'm sure you can turn on a barbecue."

"Holly, I'll help." I gripped her shoulders. "You're rambling. You've got to calm down."

She sucked in a deep breath, her chest rising. "Yep, calm."

"Sorry I'm late."

"It's okay. You texted. It's not your fault."

I would've been here sooner if I'd known she'd be so frantic, but I'd been at the studio and sometimes I got into my own little world when I was mixing. So often there was an urgency about it, because I had the sounds in my head and didn't want to risk losing them, didn't want to stop until I had the song down exactly right.

A woman stuck her head through the doorway at the far end of the hall. Holly's mom looked younger than I expected or maybe I'd hoped she'd be a few decades older than me.

"What are you two arguing about?" she asked.

Holly took my arm, leading me forward. "Oh, we were just joking around. Mom, I'd like you to meet Morgan."

I stretched out my arm for a handshake. "Lovely to meet you, Liz. I've been looking forward to tonight."

She shook my hand. "And I thought you might've been a figment of Holly's imagination!"

I laughed. "An extremely large figment."

As we wandered through the kitchen, Holly picked up her phone from the table, frowning as she stared at the black screen.

"You've let it run down again, haven't you?" her mom said.

Holly shrugged.

"Honestly, I don't know how you manage your life when you can't even keep your phone charged up," Liz said over her shoulder as she strode through the French doors.

Was that her idea of a joke? I let it go.

Out on the patio, Holly introduced me to her dad and we shook hands. Rob had a receding hairline and a friendly face. Holly's pretty hazel eyes came from her mom, but she didn't particularly look like either of her parents.

Her dad sat back down, her mom too.

"I'd better get onto the barbecue," I said.

Holly shoved a drink into my hand. "You might need a beer first."

That seemed to be what the others were drinking. I took a swig. Tasted good.

Liz held my gaze. "Holly tells me you're a record producer, that Masterson's is your studio."

"That's right."

"How long have you had the studio?"

"About ten years."

She laughed. "What? Were you twelve when you started up?"

"No, I was twenty. Big difference. Excuse me." I turned to Holly. "I reckon it's barbecue time."

The two of us stepped across the room. I bent over to turn on the gas, then switched on the barbecue.

"How'd you do that?" Holly asked quietly, her eyes wide.

"Someone had switched off the gas. You've got to turn it on first."

"Oh."

She nodded, her expression earnest, as if absorbing an important concept. Her seriousness made me smile. After the barbecue had heated up, she handed a plate of chicken for me to lay out because, apparently, this was my specialty. She took over after that, turning the chicken after it was lightly charred on one side and surrounding it with an assortment of vegetables.

We chatted to her parents while we cooked. A normal conversation, one that felt less like a job interview.

Holly pointed to the chicken. "Can you please serve this up?"

"Sure."

As soon as there was room on the barbecue, she laid down hunks of Turkish bread, then zipped into the kitchen to bring back a salad. She had the timing down pat with all the food ready at the same time.

"This is quite a feast." Sitting at the table, I served myself barbecued red peppers, eggplant, and corn on the cob. "Don't you think?"

Her dad nodded, his mouth full, while her mom ripped off a piece of lightly toasted Turkish bread.

I swallowed my first mouthful. "I don't know what you did to the chicken, Holly, but it's amazing."

She smiled. The chicken was overloaded with garlic, olive oil, and probably some other secret ingredients.

Liz reached across for the salad. "So, Morgan, you own your own house too." She motioned toward my place next door. "Very impressive."

"Thanks."

"Already you're so much better than any of Holly's previous boyfriends."

Boyfriend. I liked the sound of that, even if something didn't feel quite right.

Liz laughed. "I can't keep up with all the men in her life."

"Maybe you won't need to from now on."

I felt just like putting the woman in her place. Couldn't help myself. I looked at Holly because she was the one I cared about. She held my gaze, gave me a shy smile. I liked her smile. Always had.

After we finished eating, Holly started clearing the plates.

Her mother reached across for mine. "Here, I'll take that." Then, to Holly, "You'll drop them if you take too many at once."

I would've helped clear the table, except there were already two people doing the job so I left them to it.

After they sat back down, I asked, "Wasn't your brother meant to be coming tonight? Or did I get that wrong?"

Holly said, "He and Charlotte had something else going on tonight."

"Not *something*." Liz tossed her head back. "The Real Estate Institute Awards."

Holly's brother sold houses for a living and I'd already gathered he was very successful. His wife was a P.A. or some sort of assistant at the same agency.

"They have awards for that?" I asked.

Liz straightened. "What? You haven't heard of them? It's a big thing, highly prestigious, a huge gala affair with lots of important people. Oliver is up for an award because he's sold so many houses. His clients absolutely adore him. I'm surprised Holly hasn't told you all about him."

"It's great he's doing so well."

"Don't you have awards in your industry?"

I shrugged. "I'm not interested in winning awards. For myself, that is."

She placed a hand on her chest. "You don't want to win awards?"

"Not particularly. That's not what it's about for me. I want to do a good job, produce the best record I possibly can for each artist, and bring out that little extra something in each band."

Liz didn't look convinced.

"A lot of the bands he's recorded have won gold records," Holly said. "Does that count?"

"Oh, I think it does." Her mother laughed. "If they had an award for switching and changing jobs, Holly would be in the running!"

"Holly—" I gritted my teeth "—is a very talented drummer. Believe me, I know. I've recorded with a lot of drummers."

Liz raised her eyebrows. "Really? I thought The Merchants put her on probation for a reason. So they could back out if they needed to."

Way past the teeth-gritting stage, I gripped the Corona in one hand, balling my other hand into a fist under the table.

Guilt flooded through me because putting Holly on a trial basis had been my idea, a stupid one. And now this. From her mother. Resentment burned at the back of my throat for this woman I'd only just met.

Eyes wide, Liz put on an innocent expression. "You seem surprised. Sorry, but I thought that seemed obvious. I didn't think I'd said anything bad."

I stared at Liz. "Perhaps you don't realize just how remarkable Holly is on the drums. She's really something."

She reached across the table to cover Holly's hand with hers. "That's wonderful. I think you should make the most of it while it lasts."

She took her hand back while I took a deep breath.

"What about you, Rob?" I asked. "What do you think?"

"I agree with Liz," he said. "I think I've got a wonderful daughter."

Was that what he'd heard? It sure as shit wasn't what Liz had said. Wasn't even close.

The conversation continued—polite conversation so I

didn't have to kill Holly's mother—with lots of nodding in agreement from her father. We had another round of beers, with the exception of Liz who was driving. Holly brought out some chocolate dipped strawberries for dessert, and her mom asked me lots of questions about The Merchants. Turns out she was a huge fan, and seemed to think I was the expert on them.

"Holly has got to know them on a different level," I said. "Deeper. She's one of the guys now."

She beamed, turned to her mom. "Did I tell you about the practice gig coming up at The Swamp? It's to help me get psyched up for The Salt Flats Festival and get a feel for playing on stage with them."

It'd be Joel's first proper gig with the band too, something Holly forgot to mention.

"I'm worried about you, honey." Liz reached for Holly's hand. "Things are moving so fast. It's a big leap. Won't that be too much, too soon?"

"I'm doing okay, Mom."

"As long as you're coping. I know this is what you've always wanted, but that doesn't mean it's easy, not when it's happening all at once."

Finally Liz seemed to be showing some concern for her daughter. About time.

I looked across at her. "If anyone can do it, Holly can."

Rob held up his beer. "I'll drink to that." He knocked back the last of his beer and put the empty bottle on the table. "Might be time for us to get going."

After we walked her parents to the door, I was pleased to see Liz give Holly a hug. Her mom asked a few more questions about the upcoming gig at The Swamp, with

Rob practically dragging her away from the door while waving goodbye to us.

Holly got into automatic-mode back in the house, clearing the patio table and tidying up. I helped, but she was quiet, not saying much. I liked it better when she rambled.

I stood behind her while she deposited some dishes into the sink. "Your mom's not exactly a doting mother."

"No."

"I wish you'd told me."

She reached for a towel to wipe her hands, tossing it onto the countertop as she looked up at me, tears glimmering in her eyes.

I rubbed her arm. "I'm sorry."

"Don't worry." She smiled wanly. "I'm past crying. It can be torture talking to my mom, but some of what she says is true. Over the years, I've had lots of boyfriends. I do flit from thing to thing." She shrugged. "It's taken me a while to find my groove, that's all."

"I get it, Holly. I can see what's going on."

I saw a beautiful, funny, talented young woman with an amazing future standing in front of me and tonight I'd seen a manipulative, critical mother who loved her daughter nonetheless.

"Sad thing is my mom doesn't know the half of it," Holly said.

"We've all done stupid things when we were young."

She looked up at me, her expression pained. "That's not it. I've made some terrible mistakes where men are concerned. Stuff that goes way beyond bad." As I stared at her, she added, "Not the thing with my teacher. This was a couple of years later."

"What was?"

"My next serious relationship. He was loving at first, kind and attentive. I needed somewhere to stay and it seemed easy to move in with him. That's when I found out there's a fine line between 'attentive' and 'controlling', found he wasn't such a nice guy after all. He used to check my phone, acting suspicious as if I was having an affair or something."

My jaw tightened. I had a horrible feeling I knew where this was going, and I didn't want it to go there. I placed my hands on her little shoulders, resisting the urge to pull her close because she needed to talk, needed to get this out.

"After a while, he didn't want me going out on my own or seeing my girlfriends, Jess especially." Holly's voice cracked. "He kept chipping away at my self-confidence, made me doubt myself."

"You could see this happening at least. That's something."

"Yeah, but he made it seem so reasonable, so credible." She gasped, her shoulders stiffening beneath my hands. "He started pushing me around. Then it got more physical. He slapped me."

My pulse rising, I squeezed her shoulders too tightly, then loosened my grip. "I-I'm…"

"That was when I went to Jess. And she got me out of there."

"I'm glad."

Fear glimmered in her eyes. "The thing that scared me the most was his gun collection. Not that he threatened me, but it was enough to know the guns were there. I've read a lot about domestic violence since then. Over half the women killed each year are killed by their partners, either current or former. Some women have it a lot worse than I did."

I held her gaze. "That's no excuse for what he did."

"No, it's not."

Anger burned inside me. "What was his name?"

"That doesn't matter."

"What was his name?" I kept my voice even, my stomach surging, fury boiling in my gut.

"Jason Sutherland."

I'd never heard of the guy and maybe that was just as well. If I ever laid eyes on him, I'd beat some fucking sense into him, show him how it felt. How could he do that to Holly? To any woman?

One thing I knew, a guy like him would be looking for a victim. His sort could spot it a mile away. They thrived on the power because it made them feel like something. Holly had been younger then and growing up with a mother like hers must've eaten away at her self-confidence.

I sucked in a deep breath, letting it out slowly. "I've got to ask. What happened to him? Did you press charges?"

"No, I didn't want any trouble. Just wanted to get out. Far as I know, he still lives in Frankston but I haven't seen him for years."

"Let's hope it stays that way."

What was I doing asking questions, thinking about myself and my anger? I pulled her in and held her close. I rubbed her back, trying to make the past go away even though I knew that was never going to happen.

"I'm sorry," I said.

"It's okay," she mumbled. "Not your fault."

I held her at arm's length. "And it wasn't yours either."

She nodded, her lower lip quivering.

"I'm on your side, Holly."

Cupping her jaw in my hands, I pressed little kisses to her forehead, her temples, her eyelids. I wanted to kiss the pain and the past away and make things right.

"You're an amazing person, Holly Jacobs."

She looked up at me. "And a shit hot drummer."

"See, you can always make me smile."

Sliding her hands up behind my neck, she pulled my head down, pressing her lips against mine. I drew her in closer, held her head against my chest, stroking her soft hair. I could've held her forever.

She kissed me again, more urgently this time, her fingers tugging at the back of my hairline. Opening her mouth against mine, she deepened the kiss, and I'd be damned if there wasn't a direct line between my tongue and my groin, desire surging through me.

I wanted her. I'd wanted her since the first time I'd laid eyes on her all those years ago.

Her hands wandered over my chest, unbuttoning my shirt, then lower down to my waist. Lower still. God, how I wanted her. Suddenly the button on my jeans was undone, her hand sliding inside.

I covered her hand with mine, pulling away. I was as ready as I'd ever been, but this wasn't about me. Somehow this felt like too much, too soon after what she'd told me. I had to take care of her, make sure she was all right.

"Holly, are you sure?"

One of my hands was in hers as she stepped back, curling her index finger for me to join her. "The bedroom."

Hell, when she put it that way, who was I to argue? I followed her into the bedroom, picked her up, and lay her gently on the bed. I kissed her slowly—or at least I tried to take it slow—my hands wandering to her waist, her hips, those boobs that fit so perfectly in my hands.

I took her clothes off piece by piece. Ripped mine off as quickly as I could, then lay back down beside her. I kissed her neck, her shoulders, her nipples, taking pleasure in her moans.

I trailed my mouth lower and took my time as I went down on her. Her body writhed beneath me, her breaths increasing, tension building. I wanted to give her pleasure, wanted to make things right, wanted to give her everything she desired. She cried out as she climaxed. Exactly what I wanted.

We lay together for a while. I started kissing her again, slowly at first but 'slow' never seemed to last. We made love, and I needed this as much as she did. Maybe more.

We talked. A little. We rolled around. A lot. Eventually we sat up in bed, pillows behind us, the sheets pulled up to our waists. Her naked boobs were a distraction, I had to admit, the best distraction in the world.

Holly rested her head against my shoulder. "I never thought this could be so good."

I didn't say anything. Did she mean sex or making love or 'us'? There were a lot of ways I could take this.

One hand on her chest, she sat up straight. "I didn't mean *this*. Well, I did mean this too, but I meant a lot of things. I meant *you*. You're wonderful, Morgan. I feel like everything is falling into place for us, as if this was meant to be. I was meant to move in next door to you, and you were meant to play your music too loud, and I was meant to practice the drums outside to annoy you."

I smiled. "Has anyone ever told you you're cute when you ramble?"

"Only you."

"Then every guy who came before me was too stupid to see what was right before his eyes."

She pressed a quick kiss to my lips. "See, I was right. You. Are. Wonderful."

We didn't talk much after that. Holly was still snuggled up beside me when I heard her breathing become more rhythmic as she fell asleep. I slid my hands underneath, pulled her down the bed, and adjusted the pillows, trying not to wake her. She moaned a little, went straight back to sleep.

I lay beside her, staring at her sleeping form. So pretty, so petite, so much quieter now she was asleep. I'd expended so much energy tonight I should've been able to get straight to sleep, but sleep escaped me.

Something burned inside me, not the anger from earlier tonight, something that went deep into my core. Visions flashed in my mind, though I tried to keep them away. Juliet laughing, the pain that had shot through my heart, her face when she left me, my mother sitting me and my brother down to tell us she was leaving, my joy when she came to visit, my sadness every time she left, the devastation when she told us she was leaving for the other side of the country.

I pressed my eyes shut and tried to think about Holly, her smile, how good things were between us. Maybe she'd leave me one day too, but in the meantime we had something beautiful and I should make the most of it.

Eventually I drifted to sleep.

CHAPTER THIRTEEN

Holly

I paced backstage at The Swamp, only there wasn't a 'backstage' here. Morgan had secreted me away to the staff room at the rear of the building.

I stopped, hung my head. "I always do this."

Morgan placed his hands on my shoulders. "Do what?"

"I mess things up as soon as they start to get good." I shook my head. "I can't screw this up, I can't. There's too much riding on it."

"Good."

I stared at Morgan, shook his arms off. "Good? How can this be good?"

"If you can recognize you've got a problem, you're halfway there already."

I threw my hands up. "Great, I recognize that I'm a screw-up."

"Holly, Holly, Holly."

Nerves simmered in my stomach. "What?"

He took my hands into his. "You're not the same girl you were at nineteen. You've surrounded yourself with good people, people like Jess, like the guys in the band, and maybe like me too. You're choosing your path in life. Don't be afraid of success. It's yours for the taking."

I straightened. "Who ever said I was afraid of success?"

Morgan stared at me, didn't flinch, and maybe a little of his calm started to seep into me. Because he was right.

"I'll be okay when we start playing."

I wasn't sure where the words had come from, only that they were true. I'd done this enough times to know how it worked.

"I know you, Holly. You get knocked down, then you get right back up again."

Renewed energy surging through me, I raised a triumphant fist in the air. "I'm not on my own anymore. Together, you and me, we can conquer."

What's more, I didn't even care how dorky that sounded. I threw my arms around Morgan, then broke off the embrace, and took his hand to lead him into the bar. I was a leader. I was a good drummer, and I could do this. Besides, the anxiety in my chest was perfectly normal, nothing to worry about.

A wall of noise cut through the air as soon as I opened the door to the main bar, pulling Morgan behind me. People, lots of people. Friends of the band had been invited, then friends of friends. Word had got out.

Joel edged through the crowd. "I was looking everywhere for you. Are you okay?"

I nodded. "Never been better."

"We're on in five."

"Sure thing."

Tonight was for Joel and me, the two new members of

the band. To help us get prepared for The Flats Festival. I should be excited, not shivering with fear at the thought.

As Joel disappeared into the crowd, I squeezed Morgan's hand, the warmth of his grasp reassuring.

A raised hand in the crowd grabbed my attention. Waving. She pushed her way toward us. Mom. Smiling.

She gave me a kiss on the cheek. "I was looking everywhere for you." She pulled Dad closer. "We wanted to wish you luck."

I smiled. "Thanks."

Dad tilted his head. "Look at our little girl. Not so little anymore."

"Dad, I'm twenty-three," I said, pretending I didn't like the attention.

"And you'll always be my baby." He put his arm around me for a quick hug.

"We wouldn't have missed this for the world," Mom added.

She made me feel that's what I meant to them—the world, that is.

Morgan told them we had to go, sticking close to my side as we wove our way through the crowd. He said hello to a few people, but I didn't look around, didn't let myself get distracted, focusing only on where I was headed.

Our gear was already set up on stage and we'd had a sound check late this afternoon way before everyone had arrived. Then we'd gone home to relax, only I'd become worked up instead.

Morgan gave me a quick kiss when we reached the stage. "Knock 'em dead."

"Absolutely."

Nick reached for my hand to help me up onto the

stage. "Don't forget, your new song will be our second number tonight," Nick said.

As if I could forget. We'd practiced the crap out of the song. A good way to introduce me to the crowd, someone had said. Seemed like a good idea at the time. Not so good now.

"Sure thing," I squeaked out my response.

As I stood by the drum kit, Morgan caught my eye and blew me a kiss from the audience. Ginger crouched to one side of the stage, her camera slung around her neck ready to photograph our big night. Cooper and Austin were out there somewhere too, the old drummer and bass player.

I took a seat, waited till the other guys were ready, then snapped my sticks together for the four-count to start the opening song. Bass and guitar followed before Nick came in with the vocals, graceful at first, louder as the song started to build. Onstage magic.

He took the mic off the stand. "Thank you all for coming out tonight." A huge cheer from the audience. "We've had a couple of changes and I'd like to introduce you to the latest members of the band. First of all, here's Joel Hitchcock." Another huge cheer. He swept his arm toward me. "Now give a big welcome to Holly Jacobs."

I waved and the crowd roared, my heart surging. This was why I played, for this feeling of elation.

Nick sauntered across to hand over the mic, even though I already had one set up by the drum kit for my backing vocals.

Lachie looked at me, nodded, and strummed the guitar. It'd be just the two of us for this song. My nerves dissipated as soon as I started singing. Increasingly confident, I got up from behind the kit to stand near

Lachie. By the time it came to the chorus, I had them in the palm of my hands. More of that magic.

> *Well you are always*
> *In my dreams*
> *I hear you laughin'*
> *Or so it seems*
> *I don't know fortune, don't know fame*
> *And I don't even know your name*

The crowd cheered as the song finished. I beamed at Morgan standing at the front, clapping wildly. Ginger was taking photos as I handed Nick back the mic and made my way back to the drums, the world's biggest smile on my face.

I sat on the stool. And saw him. Jason, my old boyfriend. Shock rocketed through me, took my breath away. He caught my eye and stopped clapping, a smug look on his face. *No, it can't be.* And just like that, my past came crashing back.

Deep breaths, Holly. I looked away. Screw him, screw everything. Why now? Why tonight? No time. Hell, I couldn't get my head together, could barely get in enough air.

I missed my cue. Nick and Lachie were starting the next song, an acoustic number, and I mucked it up completely, coming in a bar late. I tried to compensate. Too late.

The audience clapped. But the guys in the band knew I'd botched up. I barely looked at them, didn't dare look at Morgan, and sure as shit didn't turn my head toward Jason.

The next song was another acoustic number, another disaster.

We moved into the rock numbers, the hard stuff that the crowd loved, and I thought it might get better. I hoped. I struggled.

I missed the stops and played where I wasn't supposed to. I came in on the on-beat instead of the off-beat. My drum fills were out of kilter, my endings sloppy, my performance a joke. The nerves in my stomach increasing with each mistake, I kept mangling song after song. Or at least that was how it felt. I was the drummer. I was supposed to be the heartbeat of the band.

Nick took control, cutting the set short and telling the crowd we were only doing one song for the encore and that they'd have to come and see us at The Flats instead.

After we finished, Morgan helped Ginger down as she stepped off the stage. Great, she'd documented one of the worst nights of my life and Cooper must be wondering what the hell was going on and why the band had taken on such a loser. I hated to think what the rest of the band must think.

Morgan reached out to me, his eyebrows going up in the middle as he pulled me down off the stage and into his arms. He didn't say anything, just held me close. The security of his embrace made me feel better. Marginally.

"You're shaking," he said.

I held back the tears burning at the back of my eyes. "I'm sorry."

He held me at arm's length. "Are you okay?"

"Yes." My voice cracked. "No."

Movement in the corner of my eye. Jason, heading in our direction. How could he? What the hell was he thinking?

Morgan gripped my arms. "Holly, what's up?"

"My old boyfriend, the one who knocked me around, th-that's him."

Morgan's expression froze, only for a moment, then he stepped between me and Jason who was suddenly upon us.

"Jason?" he asked.

He nodded. "Yeah."

Morgan smashed his fist into Jason's face. Jason reeled back, stayed standing, his hand rubbing his jaw. People on either side stopped and stared. Morgan slammed in another fist, into his gut this time. Jason doubled over. Two friends on either side held him up.

It sucked the air right out of me too, took my breath away.

Morgan pointed a finger at him. "Now we're even."

Jason scowled. "What the fuck?"

"Don't come anywhere near Holly. Got it?"

Jason's eyes narrowed. "You haven't seen the last of me. I'll make you pay, both of you. You won't even see it coming."

He spat on the floor and turned away.

Morgan stared at the back of him, then took me by the hand and led me into the back room. Breathless by the time we got there, my chest heaved with deep breaths.

He paced the small room. "Seeing him threw you tonight. That's what happened, isn't it?"

I nodded. Perspiration beaded Morgan's brow, his mouth open as he raked a hand through his hair. I'd never seen him this way before.

"I..." I didn't know what to say or what I felt.

"Have a seat."

Morgan pulled up a chair for me so I dropped down onto it, my head in my hands. I had no clue how any of this had happened. The night was such a mess I didn't even know where to start.

After a while, Morgan said, "The asshole deserved it."

"I don't care about Jason. I only care about you." I looked up at Morgan, tried to make sense of this side of him I'd never seen before. "You're not very forgiving."

His chest rose with a deep breath. "He's forgiven."

I smiled—couldn't help myself—then spluttered and covered my mouth. My pathetic splutter turned to a full blown laugh as I let off the nerves and energy pent up inside me.

Morgan shrugged, as if not sure what to make of it. A knock at the door made him turn his head, then Nick came straight in.

"Holly, are you okay?" he asked.

I nodded, didn't know why everyone was asking me that tonight. Dread filled my gut. He was probably here to tell me The Merchants were ditching me.

"I'm sorry," I said. "I sucked tonight. Big time."

Nick's mouth formed a thin line. "That's kind of why I'm here. To find out what happened."

I sighed. "Did the other guys send you here to tell me I'm out?"

He looked at me as if I were an idiot. "No, I told Lachie and Joel I'd take care of this, mostly so they could stay out there and have a good time. We're not ditching you, Holly."

Relief, was that what I felt? Or was it exhaustion?

"Morgan, do you want to tell me what's going on?" Nick turned to him.

Morgan pulled him aside and spoke to him quietly. I didn't care if he told him how Jason used to knock me around. I didn't care about much at all right now, except I did. This band meant everything to me. Morgan meant everything to me.

Nick put a hand on my shoulder. "It's okay, Holly. This was just one night, and it's over. The audience probably didn't notice anything anyway. They never do."

I stood, found my shaking legs could hold my weight, and wrapped an arm around each of them. This wasn't the end, after all.

The door opened, and Cooper walked in. A fresh wave of embarrassment washed over me, knowing he'd seen the debacle tonight too. And he, of all people, would know exactly where I'd gone wrong.

Time to take the bull by the horns. "Hi, I'm Holly."

Morgan frowned. "You guys have never met? Sorry, I didn't realize."

I turned to Cooper. "No, but I feel like I know you."

"Same here." His smile reached his eyes. "Strange gig."

"I blew it, and I'm super embarrassed."

He held a hand out. "Hey, anyone can have a bad night. I heard the recordings, Holly. I know how right you are for the band."

"You're okay with this?"

"Sure."

The load lifted from my shoulders. What a guy.

He shifted his gaze for a second. "Just one thing. I always had a feeling Morgan was never one hundred percent when it came to recording my drumming."

"I wouldn't know about that." A small lie.

"So, ah, you don't mind having two drummers at The Flats, do you?"

My eyes widened. "The two of us. On stage. That'd be amazing."

"Austin'll be there with us for a few songs too."

Their old bass player, the whole band reunited.

Morgan put his arm around me, pulling me in close, making me feel warm and secure. "The Merchants of Menace are going to be awesome at The Flats, no question about it."

Somehow tonight's rollercoaster ride made me feel like I deserved my spot in the band. I belonged here.

Most of all, I belonged with Morgan.

CHAPTER FOURTEEN

Morgan

My place, her place, any place at all. I didn't mind. I'd driven the two of us home—to my place, as it happened—because Holly was so up-and-down tonight there's no way I would've trusted her at the wheel. She didn't need drugs, didn't need alcohol. *I* was the one who needed a beer.

I handed her one too as we sat on the sun lounges by the pool, not that there was any sun at this time of night. The cool night air washed over us. God knows I needed it.

The beer hit the spot. And Holly? She'd hit the spot long ago.

"I'm glad that's over," she said.

"It's not over. It's only the beginning. But I know what you mean."

We lounged side by side, the occasional chirp of a cricket cutting through the silence, a companionable silence that I hoped meant Holly was calming down.

I understood the ups and downs of working in a creative business. Sometimes my head would be filled with sounds, and I could hear exactly how a song was going to turn out. And I'd be glued to the mixing desk.

At other times, I couldn't get the right ambiance in the studio, couldn't get anything to work. Sometimes I'd wonder what I was doing there and why anyone would have hired me. And other times I'd think I was a fucking genius.

Holly seemed to have gone through every emotion on the spectrum tonight. I'd seen the best of her and the worst of her. And tonight I'd seen the man who'd hit her. Only once, she'd said, not that that made it any better.

Good riddance to the prick. Some things I was never going to regret.

Holly put down her beer, stood up, and pulled her loose dress over her head. Or maybe it was a shirt. I could never tell what the hell she was wearing.

Any thoughts in my head disappeared, disintegrated, turned to dust. The only part of me that was thinking was my dick. Another few steps toward the pool and her bra came off. Then she bent over to remove the yoga shorts she'd worn at the gig. Magnificently naked.

The pool had steps at one end. She slid in slowly, sitting on the steps with her breasts bobbing in the water as she reclined back onto the steps.

"The water's amazing."

I ripped off my clothes and joined her. Didn't need to be asked twice. I let the water slide over me, cool or warm, I couldn't tell. I had my arm around her, her head on my chest.

"You're a mean hand with the pool filter," she said.

Sometimes I couldn't figure out the way this woman's head worked. "Yeah."

She kissed my collarbones, my shoulders, my neck. "Anything else you're good at?"

"Lots of things."

As I pulled her closer, she opened her mouth to mine and kissed me, her boobs pressed against my chest. My hands wandered over her hips and butt. What a body. I moaned. More. With Holly, I always wanted more.

Her hands wandered too, went exactly where I wanted them. She could work wonders with those little hands. And she did.

She shifted her hands to my hips, tried to push me. "Up. Sit higher." Looking up at me, she added. "Or I'm going to drown."

I did as I was told, my butt on the top step, as she went down on me and blew me away, blew me right up to heaven, maybe further.

Afterward, she snuggled her damp body up beside mine, giving me some space, some recovery time. She sure knew how to treat a guy.

After a while, we started kissing again, hands wandering again, until she suggested we move over to the sun lounges. I followed. I'd follow a naked Holly anywhere.

She pointed to the chair. "Sit."

Who was I to disobey? Holly smiled, staring at my erection. I reached for a condom from my jeans pocket while she waited to lower herself onto me. She gasped, moving slowly at first, then faster. I opened my eyes, mesmerized by the jiggle of her boobs. I reached for them. Got lost in the moment again. Holly let out a shrill gasp, tipping me over the edge into oblivion.

We lay together side by side. I had to hold her close so she didn't fall off the sun lounge because it wasn't exactly made for two. She reached for the dress she'd ripped off earlier, opening it out so it was spread across our hips.

"I can get you a towel if you like," I said.

"No, this is good." She giggled. "We're both decent now."

I pressed a kiss to her temple. "I like you being naked."

"I'm not naked." Indignant now. "I can put on my dress and then I'd be dressed and where will you be?"

"I'll be right here. I don't mind being naked."

She whacked me gently on the chest, then giggled again. Couldn't stop laughing, in fact. I held her, waited till she was done, trying to figure out what was going on with her.

After a while I said, "You're all over the place tonight, Holly. High as a kite."

She lifted her head, held my gaze. "High on life. On music. On playing live."

"Yeah, it sure was a big night."

Her lips parted, her mouth forming an O. "Imagine what I'll be like after playing The Flats. I'll be on a bigger high than tonight. Ha! You'll have to get in training for a sexual marathon after that."

I pulled her closer. "Yep, otherwise I won't be able to keep up."

I couldn't keep up with her anyway, not because she was in The Merchants heading for fame and fortune, but because she was Holly. If it wasn't the band, it'd be something else. She'd move on. She always had in the past.

Besides, women didn't hang around very long in my life, not when there were other loves in their lives and better things to do and places to go. It stung. Made my heart ache. If I thought about it. I sure as shit didn't want to think about my time with Holly coming to an end.

The trick was to make the most of things while they lasted, to enjoy every moment together because one day those moments wouldn't be there.

CHAPTER FIFTEEN

Holly

We'd wandered over to my place—or, rather, the Ashton's place—for breakfast or brunch or whatever meal of the day this was, because I'd offered to make pancakes.

I'd found the biggest bowl in the kitchen to mix up a killer-sized batch of pancakes. Jess had called earlier to ask how I felt after last night, so I invited her and Lachie over. Holding the stainless steel bowl against my stomach, I whipped the wooden spoon around, mixing in the flour and other ingredients.

No way would I let a repeat of last night's disaster happen. Ever. I'd screwed that up good and proper. The guys had been understanding, Nick especially, but they wouldn't be so cool if it happened again.

Morgan got up from the table. "Holly, what are you doing?"

I stopped, put the bowl down. "Mixing."

He gave me a stern look. "I know you had a hard night last night but I think you're taking it out on the batter."

"Well, that's why they call it batter because you've got to beat it." I lifted the spoon to check the consistency of the mixture. "It's mixed now, so it's all good."

"Come on, Holly," Morgan said. "You think Nick and Lachie have never screwed up?"

How would I know? They were the rock stars and I was the new guy in the band, only I wasn't even a guy.

I shrugged. "But their botch-ups are in the past. They've got their lives in order now and brilliant records behind them. And Joel's always had his shit together. He's a great bass play. Those guys are such a tight unit. They can rest on their laurels." I threw my free hand up. "I don't have any laurels."

Morgan covered his mouth with one hand to hide a snigger. I tried to hold back a smile, failed miserably and let out a nervous laugh.

"Don't worry," I said. "I'm not going to wallow in misery. I'm going to make pancakes."

My phone vibrated on the counter so I checked the message flashing on the screen. "Jess and Lachie are here."

"I'll get the door." Morgan left.

I placed two non-stick pans on the stove, figuring I could make a couple of batches of pancakes at once, when my phone buzzed again.

I picked up. "Hi, Mom, I'm in the middle of something. I'll have to call you back."

"Too busy for your mother?" Silence—the pointed kind—from the other end of the line. "I always make time for you."

I bit my lip. "Sorry, I can't talk right now. Bye, Mom."

"Bye, honey."

I had no clue why she'd added the 'honey' onto the end, except perhaps to rile me even more.

Sucking in a deep breath, I looked across to see Jess

approaching. She gave me a quick hug, as did Lachie, then Morgan joined in just for fun, all of which beat the hell out of talking to my mom.

"Take a seat, guys." I dropped spoonfuls of mixture onto the pans, tilted one pan to spread the pancake mix, then the other. Very clever, if I did say so myself.

"I'll make the coffee." Morgan moved across to the Nespresso machine.

I smiled. "You'd better get a move on, George Clooney."

Lachie leaned back in his chair. "This is the life. It smells great in here and we haven't even started eating."

Morgan made the coffees and brought them over. I served the first pancakes, placing them in the middle of the table for Jess and the guys to eat or fight over, whichever way it worked was fine by me. They ate and I cooked.

Lachie beamed. "I always wanted to be interviewed by *Guitar Player*. Can't believe they ignored me for so long."

Jess had told me about this, Lachie's dream come true.

"They haven't ignored you." Morgan looked up from his plate. "They've mentioned you in the magazine loads of times, tidbits and little articles."

"Being 'mentioned' isn't the same." Lachie shook his head. "I don't care about the other stuff, the features about the band in *Rolling Stone* and *Billboard*. For me, *Guitar Player* is where it's at. I've pored over every issue since I started playing guitar."

Which just went to show it didn't matter how famous you were, no matter your achievements, there was always one more thing just slightly out of your grasp.

"It's all I've been hearing about all week." Jess rolled her eyes. Then to me, "Sorry, can I give you a hand?"

"No, thanks." I brought the next round of pancakes to the table. "I've got it all under control."

Morgan turned to Lachie. "I found a woman who likes to cook. How good is that?"

"And I found one who likes kickboxing and beating me up," Lachie said.

Jess gave him a playful whack on the shoulder. "At least you're always safe when you go out with me."

"Hey." Lachie grinned. "This isn't just about me. Morgan's being interviewed too."

I turned from the stove. "Really? You didn't tell me about this."

Morgan spread his arms as if he got interviewed every day.

"Chris from *Guitar Player* wants an on-the-road interview or maybe it's a day-in-the-life, I can't remember which," Lachie said. "He arrives early morning on the day of The Flats, and wants to start the day by listening to some of the tracks at the studio and then he's gonna follow on with our headlining gig."

"Yep, just a normal day for you," I said.

Lachie shrugged. "Well, no, but that's kind of the point."

I joined them at the table, the final round of pancakes ready. Morgan brought back some orange juice from the fridge and poured it into glasses for us.

Jess said, "Since the guys are busy, I thought maybe we should go to The Flats together."

I poured maple syrup onto my pancakes. "Great idea. I'll have my own personal bodyguard."

"I'll drive," she added. "You'll probably be too nervous."

Another reason why her company would be very welcome. It reminded me of old times.

"Hey." I looked at Lachie. "Aren't you supposed to be a big rock star? Shouldn't we have a chauffeur and a limo and champagne?"

He laughed. "Who needs a chauffeur if you've got Jess?"

I smiled. "I couldn't ask for better."

My mom came to mind. I'd have to call her. The thought dragged me down. Later, I'd worry about it later.

Morgan reached across the table for my hand, giving it a reassuring squeeze. Maybe he'd seen the smile on my face turn wry or maybe he was a mind reader.

"Brett will be at The Flats," Lachie said. "He's flying in that afternoon and is dying to meet you."

I nodded. I'd spoken to their manager over the phone, but he'd been touring with another outfit in Europe so I hadn't had the chance to meet him yet. Except he wasn't their manager. He was *our* manager. So exciting.

Morgan made another round of coffee, and we talked about The Flats. Nerves simmered in my stomach. Funny how something I'd always dreamed about—something beyond my dreams, in fact—could make me so anxious. No need to be so tense, that's what I told myself.

Cooper would play a handful of songs, and I'd take care of the rest. Despite the new medication he was taking, he tired easily and wouldn't make it through the whole gig.

What's more, we had roadies to set up our two drum kits and the rest of the gear, which beat the hell out of lugging a huge kit around in my car.

"And you know Austin will be joining us for a couple of songs?" Lachie asked.

"Yep." I smiled. "There'll be quite a crowd on stage."

And fun. Hopefully it'd be fun playing with their old bass player, even if I didn't know him well.

I got it. His presence was part of the band's journey, and they wanted to include everyone. I had to admire the way they did things, their appreciation and gratitude for the position they were now in. I only hoped my drumming held up. I had a lot to live up to.

Despite my doubts, I was part of something—here, sitting at the table with my close friends, and when the four of us from the band were together too.

When it was time for Lachie and Jess to leave, Morgan walked with me to the door to see them off. Somehow he seemed to be fast replacing Jess as my best friend and I didn't even know how that'd happened.

He took my hand into his. "I should help you clean up."

"No need. It won't take me long and I've got to call my mom." Dread settled in my stomach but I knew it was better to get that over and done with.

"You'll come straight over after that?" he asked.

"Absolutely."

"You look like you need a hug."

"Sure do."

He took me into his arms and held me close. Where would I be without Morgan's hugs? Where would I be without him in my life?

I kissed him on the lips, then closed the door behind him after he left. In the kitchen, I picked up my phone only to find the battery was low. Typical.

I slumped back into my chair at the table.

Mom picked up on the second ring. "You've got time

to talk to me now, have you?”

I held the phone away from my ear. I should be able to call my own mother without having to worry about being hassled.

I sucked in a deep breath. “I wanted to thank you for coming last night. And to explain. About the gig.”

“Honey, there’s nothing to explain. I felt embarrassed watching you botch the whole thing.”

Then she did the unthinkable. She laughed. Resentment burned at the back of my throat. How could she?

“If you’re going to laugh at me, I’m hanging up,” I said.

“Sorry, I didn’t mean it that way. I was trying to make you feel better.”

My hands shook as I gripped the phone. “I expect more from you. I *need* more than this, Mom.”

“But I didn’t do anything. You were the one up on stage. Your dad and I only came along for moral support. We’ve always been behind you. You know that.” Exasperation rippled through her voice. “Everything I’ve ever said and done is for your own good.”

“No, Mom. You’re always putting me down, having a little dig at me, pointing out my flaws whereas with Oliver, you’re always singing his praises.”

“Because you’re two very different people.”

“What’s that got to do with it?”

“Oliver needs all the praise and positive feedback he can get, whereas you need a little push.”

“Is that what you call it?” I held back the tears burning at the back of my eyes. “A little push?”

“Yes, that’s what gets you going and gives you

motivation."

"No way, Mom, hold it right there." My voice cracked. "This is exactly what I'm talking about when I say I need your support."

"That's what I'm doing, supporting you so you can do your best."

I couldn't accept this. I wouldn't. And maybe I should've stood up to her years ago but she was too much like Jason, eroding my self-confidence, tearing little strips off me, keeping me down.

Meanwhile the tears I'd tried to hold back tumbled down my cheeks. I let them.

"It's got to stop, Mom." I choked out the words. "No more."

Silence at the other end of the phone.

"I don't need people in my life who are dragging me down." I looked down at the table, forced myself to keep going. "I need the people who are behind me and who give me some positive reinforcement. It's not too much to ask."

"O-okay. I'll try my best, honey."

Wiping the tears from my cheeks, I refused to let my pain show and tried to have something resembling a normal conversation.

After I hung up, I stared at the phone in my hand. We still had a long way to go, but at least we had a chance at a new beginning. Might not be much but it was something.

Letting out a long sigh, I looked around the room and stood. Screw the dishes and the cleaning up. Screw everything else. I needed Morgan. Hell, I could never have got his far without him. I flew out the door, grateful he was next door when I needed him.

More than grateful. That didn't begin to describe the emotions simmering inside me, the steadily growing yearning, the attachment and devotion.

Was it possible to fall in love so quickly? That was the thing. Morgan made me feel anything was possible.

CHAPTER SIXTEEN

Morgan

"I know I should play the full record to everyone in the band at the same time," I said. "But I wanted to play it to you first."

Holly hovered over the mixing desk beside me, her gaze flitting around the control room before looking up at me with wide eyes.

She couldn't stop beaming. "I'm honored."

"It's your record too. You're part of The Merchants and part of this album."

"Play it, play it."

We stood side by side listening to the first two songs. I looked through the window into the studio where Holly had sat behind the drum kit while we recorded, driving the songs along with her drumming.

Edging closer, I let my arm brush up against hers. Though she was right there beside me, I pressed my eyes shut, remembering how she'd looked during the recording sessions, her hair in a messy ponytail, her face scrunched in concentration as she smashed it out on the drums. How could I not have fallen in love with her?

My eyes sprung open, my heart surging, then shrinking. Hell, how had I let that happen?

I put my arm around her, waiting till the song finished. "You're at the beginning of something big with The Merchants. Your life is already starting to change. Tomorrow is the big day with The Flats, and that's only the beginning. There'll be other festivals, bigger ones, other tours."

"Nothing else is like The Flats, though. This is our town, our festival, and we do things our way."

I smiled, my happiness reaching deep inside me, thanks to everything Holly had achieved and where she was headed. Holly, it all came down to her.

"This record's going to blow people away too." I made a fist with my other hand. "I can hear it. I can feel it."

It didn't matter what happened to the two of us or to the band. When we were both long gone, the music would still be there, a legacy for future generations, sounds that moved people and gave them great pleasure.

Didn't even matter that the technology would change. Some old guys would still have the vinyl or the CD and other people would have the electronic files. Maybe not forever but for a long time.

Music endured. That was why I did this.

She turned. "I might lie down."

"That's why the sofa's there."

Placing a cushion under her head, she lay across the leather. "Is it okay if I close my eyes?"

"Sure."

I pressed 'play', then lifted her feet onto my lap so I could sit on the other end of the sofa. I'd spent hours listening to each song, adjusting the levels, getting Lachie in for some over-dubs, spending time on the details till everything was just right. I should've been tired of the album by now.

Instead, the satisfaction of a job well done coursed through me. I was never going to be sick of this record. Or Holly. If only she'd never tire of me either, but that wasn't the way things would work between us, not when she had big things ahead of her with The Merchants. This would only go one way.

Still, I'd have my music, the one thing I could rely on. My throat tightened. Who was I kidding? As if that was any substitute.

I looked across at Holly, her eyes closed, wavy hair falling back from her face, expression serene. How wonderful if it could be like this always, just the two of us, enjoying each other's company and the music. The album kept playing because I'd programmed it to do so, the songs kept coming, time kept moving on when I wanted it to stand still.

Then the first chords of the final song rang through the air. *If You Ever.*

It opened with guitar first, then Nick came in with the lyrics and the song swelled, the perfect balance of movement and melancholy, building up to the big ending—guitar, bass, drums, all going crazy with Nick's powerful vocal floating over the top.

My heart swelled too. The song wasn't perfect and that was exactly why it worked. Instead, it was human, overloaded with emotion.

Holly's eyes flickered open. "Wow."

I smiled. "You were asleep."

She sat up, sidling closer to me on the sofa. "I wasn't

asleep. I was … absorbing, you know, the sounds."

"Absorbing, yep, for sure." I pulled her closer. "That last song is a killer. Slick, yet deceptively simple."

"Morgan, I'm in love. *If You Ever* is probably the most amazing song I've ever heard. That's my drumming and this is The Merchants of Menace. Sometimes I can't believe this isn't a dream."

Yep, she was in love. With a song. With the record. And even if she loved me, it wouldn't be enough.

Pain stabbed through my chest. Actual, physical pain. Shit, what was this woman doing to me? I waited a few seconds till I had my breath back.

Pressing her hand on my chest, Holly edged herself into position beside me, her legs curled up beneath her.

She couldn't stop smiling. "The record is amazing. Did I say that before? It reminds me of The Merchants' first album, the one you produced. It's got the same rawness, but it's so sophisticated at the same time."

"Thanks. Don't forget, this is your band too."

Uncertainty glimmered in her eyes. "Is it? They haven't given me any official word about that. I mean, I think I'm in with a good chance but I don't know, not for sure."

"Holly." I took one of her hands into mine. "Remember what Nick said at the gig at The Swamp? Something about introducing the latest members of the band to the audience. It wasn't just Joel. It was you too. You're in, no doubt about it."

She bit her lip. "Do you think?"

I nodded. "Yes, I do. And tomorrow you're playing The Flats Festival."

Throwing her arms around me, she gave me a hug, and when she was done, she couldn't stop grinning.

"I can't wait to tour." She looked ready to burst. "I've toured before, playing crappy little gigs and getting paid next-to-nothing, the four of us squeezed into a van, going from town to town. Not very glamorous."

I chuckled. "Those days are behind you."

She placed a hand on my shoulder. "A tour is only temporary, though. I'll always come back. Not just me, but all the guys."

Yep, no matter what happened, I'd still see her. Nick and Lachie had come back home with the aim of spending more time in Frankston and using this as their base rather than touring non-stop.

That didn't change the fact the timing wasn't right. Holly was twenty-three whereas I was thirty and had been doing this all of my adult life.

We were at different stages. I had an established name and business. Holly was just starting out with The Merchants, starting big, wonderful things ahead of her. I couldn't have been happier for her. Not so happy for myself because I could see the end ahead.

"Who'd have thought things would go this way a couple of months ago when you moved in next door?" I said.

"Sure. But I'll always be the same person."

"The same and different. You'll never be quite the same. You've already changed."

"No, I haven't."

"You've grown and you're so much more confident now. The old Holly would've freaked or changed her mind or done something to jeopardize being in the band."

She straightened, indignant now. "No, I wouldn't." A thoughtful pause. "Well, maybe."

Perhaps she couldn't see the internal shift, changes that cut to her core and altered her as a person. When we'd first met, she needed me whereas now she was flourishing.

"You believe in yourself," I said. "And you should. Because you're amazing and you can do whatever you decide. You can take on the world with The Merchants."

She leaned her head against my shoulder. "And I'll always come back to you."

'Always' wouldn't work out the way she thought it would. We were never going to go the distance but I still hoped we'd have plenty of time ahead of us. Another record, another Flats Festival, time in Frankston, and maybe I could meet her when they were touring.

I gritted my teeth. We'd barely started out together and already I could see the end in sight when I should be making the most of what I had.

She pulled away. "You're supposed to agree."

"Yeah, sure."

"Not like that. You're supposed to mean it."

"You'll go on tour. You'll come back. I know that."

"I'll always come back, that's what I said. Always."

Something unpleasant curdled in my stomach. I didn't want to have this conversation and should've steered away from it sooner. I'd already spent way too much time thinking about the inevitable. My fault, I should've known better.

"Come on, Morgan," she said.

"*Always* is a long time."

Her mouth fell open. "What kind of response is that?"

"Forget it, Holly. Sometimes I come out with crap. We should be reveling in the record and how many people will listen to it and how good it is."

"We were, until you started being Mr. Negative."

I wished she wouldn't do this, wished she wouldn't call me cute names and make my heart squeeze. But sometimes there was no backing out.

"Do you really think the two of us will go on forever?" I asked.

"Sure, why not?"

"Happily ever after with a white picket fence?"

"Look, I'm not saying you have to marry me to save my virtue or anything. And it's not a contractual arrangement like with the record company. I'm just pointing out your negativity about this whole thing. About *us*."

"I'm being realistic."

She shook her head. "That's not what I'd call it."

"Then we'll have to agree to differ."

"Don't get all mature on me, like you know so much more than I do."

"Holly, can't you see where this is going, not now, not soon, but one day?"

"Talk about looking at things in the worst light possible."

"Which is why we shouldn't talk about this now."

She edged away, realization dawning in her eyes, her face shrouded in fear of what was to come.

I'd done this to her, handled it all wrong. She was right. I was negative, pessimistic when it came to relationships.

Her eyes narrowed. "You're dumping me. That's what you're talking about, isn't it? How can you do that? How can you even think that way when we've barely just got together?"

"I'm not dumping you."

She had it the wrong way around. Holly would grow out of the relationship and move on in her own good time. That was the way these things always worked.

"I don't want us to break up or even to argue," I said. "I'm just saying we've got some issues to iron out."

She stood up. "We? Because I don't have any issues. I've been up front with you."

"Yeah, you have."

There'd been the small matter of the fallout about 'that night' when she was nineteen but we'd gotten over that pretty quickly.

She moved between me and the mixing desk, her chest heaving. "I'm not Juliet."

Pain sliced through me like a knife. I stopped myself from doubling over. One big argument between me and Juliet, and it'd all been over. One big revelation. She hadn't wanted us to spend our lives together and sure as shit hadn't wanted to have a baby with me. So she'd taken care of it, and left a huge gaping hole in my heart, left me reeling, grieving on my own. And lost. I'd never been so lost.

A different woman, a time that had been and gone, and a very specific set of circumstances. This was Holly. This was now.

I held her gaze. "I never said you were like her."

She gritted her teeth. "Yes, you did. Good enough as. You're putting me in the same category as her, and I'm not her. I'm me."

Tears filled Holly's eyes, tears that deepened my pain. I got up and placed my hands on her arms but she shook me off.

Fear skittered along my nerve endings—at what I'd done, how much I had to lose and the obvious agony I was putting her through.

"You're so unforgiving," she blurted out. "And I haven't even done anything."

I brushed the tears from her cheek. She flinched, moved back so she was butted up against the mixing desk. More than ever, I wanted to take her into my arms, hold her, and give the reassurance she needed.

For her, for me, for us. Because there should be a 'two of us' and because I couldn't bear to see her hurting like this.

My arms opening, I edged closer but she pushed me away, leaning backward over the mixing desk. I didn't want to cage her in or force her. I couldn't, not after what she'd been through with that prick, Jason.

So I stepped back, the hardest thing I'd ever had to do.

"Holly, I'm the one who's sorry."

Her face reddened. "Morgan, you're holding back."

That was where she was mistaken. I should've held back, that was the problem.

"I've done this all wrong," I said.

She circled away, her back to the door now. "That's not good enough. You're holding part of yourself in reserve, like some sort of self-protection mechanism to stop yourself from getting hurt. Well, I've got news for you. We all get hurt sometimes. That's life."

"That's not quite true."

"I'm the opposite." Her voice cracked. "I'm always putting myself out there, trying stuff, doing dumb things, and maybe it doesn't always go my way, but so what? This is life. We're supposed to be living, not just existing. I'm like that puppy that someone kicks but he always goes running back to his master. No one can keep me down, whereas you… You're Mr. Successful-And-I'm-Not-Going-To-Change-Anything. Maybe you should try some of this personal growth stuff yourself."

I stepped closer. "Holly, you believe in yourself and that's a wonderful thing."

She took my hand into both of hers, tears pooling in her eyes all over again, and she lifted my hand to her chest, her heart beating beneath my palm.

"Believe in me," she said. "Believe in *us*."

"I believe in you, Holly. I have for a long time."

She let my hand drop, her lips parting as she took a small step back. Not the answer she wanted. Horror filled me because I couldn't bear for things to go this way, yet I couldn't say the words she needed to hear.

Turning away, she swept her purse from the mixing desk and pulled open the door.

"Holly, wait."

She stopped. We'd come here together in my car, and maybe she'd just realized that.

"Let me drive you," I said.

"The least you can do is let me storm out of the room." She turned and glared. "Don't come after me, Morgan. Don't you dare."

I watched her leave, then slumped down onto a chair, my head in my hands. What had I done? What kind of shit-for-brains idiot was I?

CHAPTER SEVENTEEN

Holly

Morgan had knocked on my front door last night but I'd refused to answer, hadn't been able to see him so soon. Or speak to him. Hadn't been able to pick up the phone either, so we were reduced to texting.

So where did that leave us?

I sighed, stepped in front of Jess who was waiting on the sofa in the living room which wasn't my living room, or it wouldn't be after the Ashtons returned from vacation.

"How does this look?" I asked.

"Looks great." She frowned. "Have you lost weight?"

Words most women would love to hear, but not me. I didn't need to lose weight. And it wasn't possible I'd lost weight overnight anyway.

I'd stressed about what to wear and had changed outfits several times, which was very unlike me. As much as I wanted to wear jeans, even at night it'd be too hot up under the lights. I'd ended up with a pair of denim shorts—knee-length for modesty on stage, with a couple of rips for the cool factor—and a black tank, failsafe.

Jess pointed. "That's some bra you're wearing."

"I'll take that as a compliment."

A running joke between us because Jess always made sure she had sturdy support for training and when she was on the job, whereas I didn't care if I went around braless. Except on stage. Then I cared. A lot.

"Maybe I should put the red tee back on," I said. "For a bit of color on stage."

Jess stood. "Nope, you're not getting changed again."

I frowned, could've fussed, could've insisted. "Is it time to go?"

"That's what I've been trying to tell you."

In a strange way, last night's argument had given me something to worry about other than the gig tonight, made me less nervous, distracted me. But this wasn't a normal gig. It was a concert, and we were headlining. The other bands had played over the weekend, and the crowd would be waiting for The Merchants.

Forget about being distracted. A fresh wave of nerves shot through me.

I threw my arms around Jess, and she hugged me.

"You'll be fine." She smiled, holding me at arm's length. "In fact, you'll be fantastic."

"Thanks for hanging around today."

She picked up her purse, slung it over her shoulder. "No problem. It's not as though I had anything better to do."

That wasn't sarcasm on Jess's part. Lachie had spent the day with the guy from *Guitar Player*. And with Morgan. Which had left Jess and me free.

I'd told her what had happened with me and Morgan, going through every detail and recounting the conversation practically word for word. Joining The Merchants wasn't supposed to be at the cost of losing Morgan. It wasn't supposed to work this way. I'd cried and ranted a bit—or a lot—and she'd fumed on my part. That's what friends were for.

Then I'd dredged up a smile and forced myself to stop thinking that way. As much as it sucked, I had to pull myself together. People out there were depending on me and I couldn't let anyone else down.

"Are you ready?" she asked.

I grabbed my bag. I'd already packed the important things: several sets of my favorite brand of drumsticks, a sweat towel, some spare clothes, and a frozen water bottle. There'd be plenty of water backstage, of course, but I was used to bringing my own.

The sound of sirens assailed us as soon as we stepped out the front door, a police car speeding by, lights flashing against the night sky, then another.

"I wonder what's going on," I said.

Jess motioned for me to get in the car. "We can find out later."

We had an hour's drive ahead of us. Jess had already checked out the route ahead of time and found out about the backstage entry because that's the sort of thing she always did, whereas I'd have been more likely to wing it.

I tried to Zen out by taking deep breaths while Jess drove, and it worked. A little, at least. Wondering if Morgan had texted, I dug the phone out of my bag.

"Dead." I looked down at it. "Just my luck. Can I use your charger?"

"Nope," she said. "My phone is still charging. We've got a long drive ahead of us. Plenty of time."

"Sure."

Her phone was face down on the console between us, set on silent and non-vibrate because that was her default setting. She even refused to place it on speakerphone unless she was on a job and absolutely had to. Too much of a distraction, according to her.

"You shouldn't be hanging out for a message from Morgan," Jess said.

"I'm not." A tiny lie.

"You'll be seeing him soon enough anyway."

I drummed my fingers on my thigh. Yep, very Zen. "I *need* my phone."

"You're not going to need it on stage."

"No, but I'm going to need some valium to calm me down."

She gripped the wheel. "You know what we could try instead of a tranquilizer? A conversation, you know, like two friends who've known each other for years might have."

"We could try it. See what happens. I'm not going to talk about Morgan, though. I've talked about him enough."

"Yep, you're doing an excellent job of not mentioning him at all."

I let out a nervous laugh. Jess smiled as she drove.

If only I was smiling on the inside. If only I could go back in time so last night had never happened. Or perhaps fast-forward to tomorrow when I'd already played The Flats and my nerves were over and done with.

But I couldn't wish my time away. Life was way too precious.

CHAPTER EIGHTEEN

Morgan

To text or not to text, that was the question.

I'd already messaged Holly a couple of times. Maybe I should just call her but she hadn't picked up my previous calls and I had no reason to believe she'd pick up now. I couldn't blame her.

Chris was sitting on a table in the backstage marquee, feet dangling, while Lachie and I sat on the only two chairs. The day had flown by. It helped that Chris was a hell of a nice guy and genuinely interested in everything to do with guitars and Lachie's guitar playing in particular. Made it feel more like we were spending time with a friend than a journalist.

"Do you have any rituals, anything you do for good luck before a gig?" he asked.

"Not really." Lachie shrugged. "It's one of those things. There's lots of waiting around, no way round it."

"Don't you guys all usually hang together?"

"Yeah, usually," Lachie said.

The other guys were in a different marquee, one we'd dubbed 'the party tent," lit up like a 24-hour grocery store in the middle of the night. Lachie had a headache so we'd found the quietest place we could, not that anything around here was particularly quiet.

One of the roadies appeared in the doorway, an older guy called Doug who was weathered from too much time on the road. Phone clenched in his hand, arms at his sides, his eyes darted from person to person, sweat beading on his forehead.

"Hi, guys," he said. "Is Holly here?"

Lachie shook his head. "No, she's on her way with Jess."

"Both of them? You sure?"

"Yeah, I'm sure. Where else would she be?"

"Have either of you talked to Holly, you know, in the last hour?"

Lachie frowned. "What is this, twenty questions?"

Doug swallowed, stepped closer. "I don't know how to say this."

A shiver shot up my spine, my skin suddenly turning cold. The argument with Holly, her not answering her phone, a car crash on the highway, all the worst thoughts flashed in my mind.

"Just come out with it," I said.

"I picked up Holly's drum kit from her house this afternoon. She and Jess were both there. We had a bit of a chat. They're really nice girls."

"And?" I asked.

"There's been a shooting." Doug's mouth stayed open, his brow furrowed, eyes hooded over. "I saw the news on my phone and came to find you right away."

"A shooting?" I croaked, not sure if the words had come out.

He nodded. "In Bedford."

That was where I lived, where Holly lived. Holly…

My chest seizing up, I stood on shaking legs. Lachie got up too.

"In Bedford?" I repeated.

"Reports said the victim was a young woman living alone. Shot through the chest, that's all I know."

Shot through the chest. The breath left my body. But, no, I didn't know it was Holly. Could be just a coincidence.

"Th-they've cordoned off Abbott Road," Doug added.

The street where I lived. Where Holly lived. My heart clenched, my world falling apart, a hundred regrets rocketing through me.

"Let me have your phone." I snatched it from his hand, then passed it back. I had my own damn phone and I was on it in a flash, only it was like a bad dream where my thumbprint ID wouldn't work, my fingers fumbled, and I couldn't even type in the passcode. My worst nightmare.

Fuck.

I looked across at Lachie, his face ashen, eyes lowered to his own phone. Was he having the same problem as me?

What to do? Race back to Bedford to find them? Should I call the police first, and what would they tell me anyway?

Fuck.

"Last time I heard from Jess was over an hour ago," Lachie mumbled, his head down, hair hanging over his face. "She texted to say they'd be leaving Holly's house soon."

"They hadn't left yet?"

"No."

Still back at home, not in the car safely on their way. A fresh wave of anxiety shot through me.

Maybe I should've been thinking about Jess too, not only Holly. It could've been either of them. Or both. Or neither.

I couldn't breathe, couldn't think, and I was having trouble getting my fingers to obey. I'd made the biggest mistake of my life with Holly. I had to make it up to her. I had to.

Chris slid off the table where he'd been sitting, his gaze fixed to his phone. "I found something. They've made an arrest. An estranged husband or partner, they say, the name not yet released."

"Okay." Lachie's voice shook. "Then it's p-probably not them."

I froze. An aggrieved ex, Holly had one of those, a guy who'd abused her, who had a gun collection.

His words came back to me—*I'll make you pay, both of you. You won't even see it coming.*

Maybe Holly had damn good reason to be scared of the guy.

And I'd punched him out, aggravated him, opened up old wounds.

Fuck, fuck, fuck.

Fear cut through me, sinking deep into my bones. If anything happened to Holly, I'd never forgive myself.

Passcode, Phone, Recents, finally I pressed the buttons to get through to Holly. The phone rang. Went to voice mail. Panic surging through my veins, the words tumbled out in a frenzy.

"Holly, call me. It's urgent. I love you."

I hung up. Why couldn't she pick up her phone? Why?

What if something terrible had happened to her and my final words to her were the ones spoken last night? I couldn't bear it.

My chest felt like it'd been cut open, my heart exposed, a great gaping wound that was ripping me open.

How could I have been such an idiot and not seen what was right in front of me? What the hell had I been thinking? I couldn't lose her. I couldn't.

Looking across, I saw Lachie had his phone to his ear, speaking into it. He pressed a button on his phone, shook his head. No, he hadn't got through either.

I paced the floor. I had to do something, but what? What do you do when you think the love of your life has been shot?

"Holly, are you okay?" Lachie's voice.

He'd got through to them. That had to be it. Dread gripped my heart, fear that I might be wrong.

"And Jess? What about her?" Lachie looked up at me and nodded. "They're both fine."

I slumped back into the chair. Relieved, anxious, calmer, more frenzied than before. I had no idea of the emotions coursing through me. Lachie spoke into the phone, his words floating in the air, but not a lot was sinking in.

A few moments or a few minutes later—I had no idea which—I stood and held my hand out to Lachie. "The phone, I need your phone."

"Hold on," Lachie said, then handed it to me.

I took it. "Holly, is that you? Are you okay?"

As Lachie stepped back as if to get some air, Chris handed him a bottle of water, a hand on his shoulder.

"I'm fine." Holly's voice. That was really her.

"You're fine." My mouth dry, I could barely speak.

"What's going on? I couldn't figure out what Lachie was saying."

"Where are you?" I asked.

"We're probably about fifteen minutes away."

"What happened to your phone?"

"It ran out of juice."

"Morgan, you haven't told me what's going on."

Chris unscrewed the lid of a bottle of water and shoved it into my free hand. A mind reader. I drank a mouthful. My mouth was still dry but I started talking, told Holly what had happened. What we'd feared.

Maybe we'd jumped to conclusions. I didn't give a shit. Holly was on her way and she was okay and nothing else mattered.

*   *   *

Lachie and I waited next to the chain link fence by the boundary. The inside of the fence was lined with black plastic so no one could see in, the gate guarded by several security guys.

We'd already teed up Holly and Jess's entry with the head of security to ensure smooth access. Somehow I seemed to be able to get my brain functioning properly again after I'd found out Holly was okay.

On our way to the rear gate, we'd stopped to explain to the other guys what'd happened. I don't think they quite got it, and maybe you wouldn't unless you were in our situation. Maybe it'd sink in later.

Chris had stayed behind with the guys. He'd seen the looks on our faces and had understood well and truly, but hadn't interfered. This would probably end up in his article as some sort of exclusive, not that I cared much either way. Right now Holly was the only thing I care about.

Meanwhile Lachie and I waited for Holly and Jess.

Waiting.

I fluctuated between pacing and shoving my hands into my pockets. No one else tried to talk to us, thank God, probably because the looks on our faces were so dire.

One of the security guards pressed his fingers to his earpiece and nodded at Lachie, then he and another guy pulled open the gate.

Jess strode in first, her right arm hidden behind her as she pulled someone through the gate. Holly stumbled along behind her.

Holly. It had always been Holly.

CHAPTER NINETEEN

Holly

Morgan swept me in to his arms and spun me around, made me feel like a teenager again, then lowered me slowly to the ground, his grasp firm as if reluctant to let go. I didn't want him to let go either. I wanted to stay like this always.

He kept his arms wrapped around me. "I'm so glad you're safe."

"We were never in any danger." I nuzzled into his chest, firm and reassuring.

"But I thought you were." He broke the embrace and looked into my eyes. "That's the whole point. I *thought* you were gone. Thought you were … dead."

I smiled. "I-I'm not."

"I was scared, Holly, and that's not something I'd normally admit to." Cupping my jaw in his hands, he kissed me slowly, delicately. "I've never been so happy to see someone in my life."

It was starting to sink in. In the car, I'd been confused. As far as I'd been concerned we were on our way to the gig and it had all seemed like a weird misunderstanding, but maybe none of that mattered. Morgan's feelings mattered, his feelings for me.

"Let's get out of the way." He took my hand, pulled me to one side so we weren't blocking the gate.

Jess and Lachie stood not far from us, all wrapped up together in their own little world. I knew exactly how they felt.

"It's not your fault, Holly. None of this is your fault. It's me, I screwed up. This has made me realize how important you are. You're everything to me, Holly, and I don't want to lose you."

"I'm not going anywhere, except maybe up on stage." My stomach fluttered like crazy, perhaps because of Morgan, perhaps because of the gig. "It's nearly time. I need to get ready."

He pressed a kiss to my forehead. "You should play your heart out tonight, but leave some space in your heart for me."

Somehow having Morgan here made everything seem better. He and Lachie knew exactly where to go. It was tent city back here, so different from backstage at the grungy bars I'd played at. Not that this was glamorous, far from it.

We found the marquee with the other guys and had a round of hugs. There was lots of talking-on-top-of-each-other and people checking that Jess and I were both okay. Quite a crowd had gathered—all the guys from The Merchants, including their old bass player and drummer and girlfriends. People everywhere. Crowded yet somehow comfortable.

I couldn't figure out what was happening. Time stood still, then surged ahead on fast-forward. Like a dream? Was that what this was?

Roadies came and went, taking short breaks between setting up on stage. In the distance we heard the roar of the crowd, then the music stopped. I only noticed the previous band when they stopped playing. It wasn't silence, not exactly. It felt like the quiet before the storm and we were the storm.

Someone said we were on. My pulse raced. Could this really be happening? Morgan took my hand, leading me to the side of the stage. The other guys were grinning. I had a few sets of drumsticks in my back pocket. Did I need anything else?

More waiting. Always so much waiting.

Morgan's arm hadn't moved, so reassuring. My eyes adjusted to the light. Roadies moved across the darkened stage. I didn't dare shift my gaze toward the crowd. I could hear them. Restless, like a sleeping animal.

Nick came up beside me. "We're on in a sec. You know the deal. Cooper will play the first few songs, then you'll join us on stage straight after that."

I stared at the two drum kits on stage, my Gretsch kit gleaming in white marine pearl and Cooper's kit set up closer to me.

"Sure," I said.

"You're nervous."

"I-I've never played in front of so many people before."

Nick nodded toward the audience, waving it off. "They're just lots of little faces, so small in the distance. You go out there and do your thing."

Though not convinced, I nodded. "Okay."

Morgan pulled me closer. "Those people are here

because they want to see you and because they love you."

I swallowed. "They don't know me."

"But they will. After you start playing, they'll feel like they know you, and that's all that matters."

Nick and the other guys went on stage and played those first few songs with Cooper just like we planned, while I watched from the sidelines. Such a strange out of body experience. As if I was looking down on Morgan and myself, then looking out at the band from a height. I was there, and I wasn't.

Then it hit me. This was my band. This was my life.

And I had Morgan at my side.

Lachie finished the song with a huge guitar solo. The crowd went wild.

Ginger took photos from the sidelines. Of the band, the crowd, of me and Morgan.

At the front of the stage, Nick tossed his head back, long hair flying. "Ladies and gentlemen, let's hear it for Lachie Tyler." He waited till the crowd calmed down, then held his arm out in the other direction. "Give a big welcome to our new bass player, Joel Hitchcock."

The crowd roared. Joel waved, then rested his right hand on top of his bass as if he'd been doing this all his life.

Nick pushed his hair back behind his ears. "But wait. There's more." The crowd lulled. They always listened to him. "Don't forget about Cooper on drums."

Cooper smashed out a quick drum roll, then stood up behind his kit.

"Frankston, you don't know how lucky you are!" Nick yelled. "Because Cooper is staying right here in town."

My cue to go on. Morgan pressed a kiss to my cheek,

then let me go. The crowd got revved up all over again. I waved at Morgan as I left, striding onto the stage.

"Now let's welcome Holly Jacobs." Nick made a huge show of it as he bowed to me, then turned back to the audience. "Not only is Holly the newest member of the band, she's our secret weapon."

Cooper gave me a quick kiss as he left the stage and I headed for my drum kit, the roar of the crowd ringing in my ears, blood pumping, stomach surging.

I held Morgan's gaze as he stood at the side of the stage, an eerie calm taking over. I had Morgan, and I couldn't want more. Thousands of people out there in the audience and I was thinking about the one person who mattered the most, my heart filled with satisfaction and love. Yep, I was pretty sure that was love.

Nick let out a devil's scream to open the next song and I came in with the drums and we were off. Song after song after song.

Every time Nick spoke to the crowd between songs, they went wild. They loved him. Loved *us*. Didn't matter what he said or did, they lapped it up.

"I've got the best job in the world," he said into the microphone.

So did I. I looked across at Morgan. I could add to that, the best boyfriend, the best life.

Nick shook the hair from his face. "I've also got the best guitar, thanks to the kind folks at Gibson for the Nick Steel Signature Guitar. You guys are the first ones to see this baby!"

The crowd roared again. My parents and brother were out there in the audience somewhere. I'd given them backstage passes and would probably see them later.

Meanwhile there was only now. My heart swelled, my body light as we started the next song, only for me to be carried away on the biggest wave of my life. And I didn't even surf.

Nick waited for the clapping to die down. "Can I have your attention please?" He strummed his new guitar softly and kept talking. "Thank you all for coming tonight. You guys are special to us. Frankston is special to us. And playing The Flats … I can only say *wow*." More clapping.

He waited, then said, "For us, this concert was all about family and coming home. Family isn't always about blood. It's about the people in your life who want you in theirs, the ones who accept you for who you are, the ones who'd do anything to see you smile and who stand by you, no matter what."

I glanced across at Morgan, arms crossed, smiling by the side of the stage. I'd chosen him and he'd chosen me.

"We've got one more member of the family." Nick motioned toward Austin waiting in the sidelines. He strode onto the stage, waving to the crowd, as a roadie passed his double bass across to him.

"You might've seen Austin on stage earlier with his band, The Detonators," Nick said. "He's one of us too. These people on stage, these are my people. I love these guys."

And we hit it. Joel held back on bass to make room for Austin. We grooved. We rocked. The song built up to a huge wall of noise, drums, guitar, bass, Nick screaming at the front. Then suddenly we were done.

"Thank you, Frankston," Nick said. "You've been a wonderful audience. The best."

Waving at the crowd, we headed off stage. My heart

was racing as I reached Morgan. He put his arm around me, didn't say anything, which was exactly what I needed.

The crowd was having none of it. Whistles, cheering, shouting, then chanting. *Mer-chants, Mer-chants.*

Nick grinned. "Let's put them out of their misery."

We tramped back on stage for the songs we were saving for last. *If You Ever.* My first ever encore.

The first time Nick had played the song, it brought tears to my eyes. I still had those same emotions inside, only they were coming out through my drumming. I held back in the quiet parts of the song, then came in hard for the chorus.

What a song, what a performance, and suddenly it was over, the crowd roaring, my body pulsing from the gig.

"Come on, guys." Nick turned and waved at us. "Let's have everybody up here."

I got up and made my way to the front of the stage, my legs suddenly shaking as the audience loomed closer. Joel put his arm around me, ushering me ahead so I stood between him and Nick, Lachie on the other side. Cooper and Austin joined us, standing on the other side of Joel, all of us grinning and waving to the crowd.

Nick stepped forward to the mic. "Goodnight, Frankston. Get home safely and we'll see you all next time."

The end of the performance.

The beginning of something big.

We edged away from the front of the stage. I walked, my eyes glued to Morgan, then ran into his arms.

Where I belonged.

CHAPTER TWENTY

Morgan

I was buzzing after the gig, and I hadn't even played. How crazy was that?

The party tent had filled with people, guys from other bands, roadies who worked hard and deserved to drink hard too, assorted hangers-on, the guys from the band, of course. And Holly, always Holly.

I didn't want to share her tonight, not after what had happened earlier, but I also couldn't drag her away when she was still on a high. This was her big night. Mine too, in some ways.

"Brett." I opened my arms to give him a hug, a difficult thing to do when that meant letting go of Holly. "Good to see you."

The Merchants' manager had been conspicuously absent with a new project on his hands, and the guys had been happy to leave him to it while they were recording and preparing for The Flats.

"We only flew in this afternoon." Brett's gaze shifted to Holly. "Nice to meet you. About time, actually."

She shook his hand, looking very professional except

for the fact she was a sweaty mess, her skin glowing, tank top stuck to those shapely boobs. Not that I was looking. Much.

Tilting her head, she frowned. "You don't look like a band manager."

Brett laughed. "Neither do you. I hear you used to be one."

"Yeah, but I wasn't very good so that doesn't count!"

I took her hand into mine. "That's telling him."

"Well, it's the truth." She paused. "But I'm a good drummer."

"You are." Brett nodded. "I'd like to take the two of you out to dinner one night this week to get to know you better."

I raised my eyebrows. "But you already know me, and the guys have probably already told you all about Holly."

He brought her free hand to his lips and kissed the back of it. "Which is exactly why I want to find out more."

Holly smiled. "Fabulous, we'd love to."

"The new album is an absolute killer," I said. "It'll be the biggest one yet, no doubt about it."

"And no doubt you've done a brilliant job." Brett turned his attention to me. "I've heard the recordings but I'd really like to run through them with you in the studio."

I nodded. "Sure thing."

Someone tapped Brett on the shoulder so he turned and greeted the other person. At the same time, Cooper and Ginger appeared, both of them with water bottles in their hands.

I gave him a fist bump. "Cooper, how're you doing, my man?"

He shook the long hair from his face. "I get asked that a lot."

"Because we care, Coops."

"I get it. I really do. And I'm feeling better than I have in a long time."

A pang shot through my heart every time I thought about Cooper's illness. At least he wasn't going through it alone. He had Ginger. And the rest of us too.

"I've got a few years in me yet," he said. "Wonderful years. Interesting ones."

He smiled, couldn't stop grinning.

I looked at Ginger, also grinning, then back at Cooper. "What's up?"

"There's something I haven't told you," he began. I hated to think he had more bad news but that wasn't what the look on his face was saying.

"What?"

He pulled Ginger close. "We're having a baby."

It took a moment for this to sink in. "You're..."

Cooper's grin took over his whole face. "Ginger's pregnant."

Holly threw her arms around Ginger, the two of them hugging while I whacked Cooper on the shoulder and congratulated him.

"Wow, that's big news," I said.

Ginger placed a hand on her flat stomach. "No, at the moment, it's quite small."

"I'm so pleased for you," Holly said, then turned to Cooper. "For both of you."

She wiped a tear from her cheek.

I put my arm around her. "Holly, you're crying."

"No, I'm not." She wiped her other cheek, letting out

a nervous giggle. "Crying is for sad people. I'm so happy for you."

"We're pretty darned happy too!" Ginger shrieked.

Nick appeared out of nowhere, his eyes wide. "Did you just say what I thought you said?"

Ginger nodded.

He kissed her on the cheek, then starting yelling about champagne, more champagne, which made me smile because I somehow doubted Ginger would be drinking much if at all.

The commotion continued, and we talked to the others, Joel and Scarlett, Austin and Tara, and Jess and Lachie, of course. People came and people went, and I made sure Holly was at my side. Tonight of all nights, I wanted to keep her close.

The shock from earlier tonight hadn't left me. It'd shaken some sense into me, though. We all had one life. We got one chance. Why screw things up? Why not live life on eleven instead?

I had to think more about Holly and less about myself. She was better than ten out of ten. She was my eleven, my reason for living, my everything.

I pulled her closer. "Maybe it's time to get going."

She looked up at me, her hazel eyes wide. "The Flats has been unbelievable. I don't want tonight to end."

I did. I wanted it to end with Holly lying beside me, her hair splayed across the pillow, my arms wrapped around her.

"Let's get some fresh air." She took my hand into hers. "For a bit of quiet. And maybe something else."

I followed her outside. The bouncers at the door nodded as we stepped around the corner where it was fractionally quieter, though the tent walls were hardly soundproof. Not the most romantic surroundings but when I had Holly, none of that mattered.

The cold night air bit into my skin, so cool it made Holly shiver. I slid my arms around her, drawing her closer.

"You're cold," I said.

She smiled. "And clammy."

"You could never be clammy."

"I'm not perfect."

"Perfect is boring. And you could never be boring, Holly."

I pressed a gentle kiss to her lips, then pulled back, sensing hesitation on her part.

"Is everything okay?" I asked.

She nodded, albeit reluctantly. "There's something you said in your phone message, the one you left when Jess and I were driving here."

"I was frantic. I'd never been so scared in my life. I thought you'd been shot."

"You said *I love you.*"

I drew her closer. "I do. I love you, Holly. I didn't say that because I was scared. I said it because it's true."

Her eyes widened, her lower lip trembling, her shoulders shaking beneath my grasp. Sometimes she felt so petite that I thought she might break.

"Holly…"

"I love you too, Morgan," she blurted the words out. "Even if sometimes you're a giant poo poo."

"Hey, them's fighting words." I wrapped my arms around her, held her tight. "And I think we've done enough fighting."

CHAPTER TWENTY-ONE

Holly

I'd woken to find Morgan's body spooned against the back of mine, warm and comfortable and cozy. Awake already, he'd been hesitant about moving in case he woke me.

Had that only been an hour ago? I had no clue.

The sun on my back, I stood by the edge of the pool, my toes overhanging as I contemplated the shimmering blue water. Last night had been so huge in so many ways that I didn't feel I had my feet back on the ground. Or my head in order.

I lifted my gaze to the far end of the pool where Morgan was seated on the steps, his hair wet, drops of water gleaming on his chest.

Sometimes there was only one way. I dove in, the cool water giving my body a jolt and clearing my head.

I swam to the far edge and pulled myself onto the steps, catching my breath, while Morgan remained strangely calm and quiet.

"Waiting for me?" I asked.

"All my life."

"That's not true."

He took my hand into his. "It's always been you, Holly. I just didn't see it any sooner."

Me neither. I hadn't seen it sooner, hadn't trusted my own judgment, had always somehow felt I wasn't good enough. Instead my heart was flooded with different feelings—of love and longing, of hope for the future. There was only one way Morgan and I could go. Together. That was the only way.

"Do you like the pool?" he asked.

"Sure, and I've got my very own pool guy! I hear you're a mean hand at fixing a pool filter."

"So you like my place?"

Was he kidding? Morgan was here, what more could I want? I may not have given the pool much thought but I coveted a kitchen like his. I'd practically fallen in love with it when I'd first walked into his place. And into his life.

Actually, the thing I ached for wasn't a thing. It was Morgan, sitting beside me. Moments ago I'd felt so certain of everything, yet now a wave of uncertainty rippled through me. So many wonderful things in my life, Morgan, The Merchants, yet one item was very much up in the air.

"Such a shame I won't always be living next door to you," I said.

"I've been thinking about that. You should move in with me."

My mouth fell open. My heart swelled at the thought but the words wouldn't come out.

"Look, if you still want to find your own place, that's okay," he said. "But that's not what I want. I want to keep you close. I don't ever want to let you go. Holly, I want you to stay. For as long as you want to stay. Forever."

I swallowed the lump in my throat. "Forever is a long time."

"I hope so."

He leaned closer and pressed a gentle kiss to my lips because 'gentle' was what I needed now. Maybe he'd want kids one day too. I sure as hell did. But it was one thing at a time.

"I love you," he said.

Bursting on the inside, I smiled. "Love you too."

One thing was for sure. This would never get boring.

ACKNOWLEDGMENTS

First of all, a big thanks to my very own rock star and in-house consultant, James.

Thanks very much to the people I interviewed, all experts in your particular fields and very patient with my dumb questions—Jenny Kim, Brooke Lundy, Scott Wilson, Brendan Murphy and Jo Taylor. Thanks heaps, guys!

And of course thanks to my fabulous critique partners, Claire, Lorraine, Juanita, Teena and Anna.

ABOUT THE AUTHOR

Susanna Rogers is the author of rock star romances for adults and kick butt books for young adults. Inspired by her very own in-house rock star and years of going to gigs, she penned the Mosh Series after writing and releasing several young adult novels. She's also a kickboxer and dreams of empowering girls and guys around the globe to believe in themselves, to take care and follow their own dreams. She has a soft spot for romantic suspense, also with kick butt heroines, so you never know what might be coming up next.

She would love to hear from you—susannarogers.com.

If you like her books, please post a review on Amazon or Goodreads. She'd like that a lot.